Saltwater Memories

P r e s s

Pittsburgh

SALTWATER MEMORIES

ANJ Press, First edition. JUNE 2021.

Copyright © 2021 Amelia Addler.

Written by Amelia Addler.

Cover design by Charmaine Ross at CharmaineRoss.com

Maps by Nate Taylor at IllustratorNate.com

For the struggles that beget strength

Recap and Introduction to
Saltwater Memories

Our story began when Mike gifted his little sister Margie a property on San Juan Island. She turned it into a wedding and events business, as well as a new home for her adult children Tiffany, Jade, and Connor. When the Chief Deputy Sheriff in town, Hank Kowalski, fell head over heels in love with her, she was surprised and delighted to accept his hand in marriage.

All the while, Mike was out of sight, working for the FBI as an undercover agent in the Koval mafia family. He thought that his family was safe from his dangerous job until he discovered that a rival mob family, the Sabinis, funded a bizarre zombie movie on San Juan Island.

After Mike showed up on the island to investigate, he accidentally caught the interest of one of Sabini's less-than-bright soldiers, Lenny Davies. Lenny took it upon himself to go looking for Mike – and ended up breaking into Margie's house as part of the process.

Luckily, Chief Hank's daughter Amanda had moved to the island to help Margie and Hank recover from their moped accident, and she was in Margie's house at the time of the break-in. Amanda tasered Lenny before he was able to harm anyone, and he was arrested, seemingly relieving the Clifton family of any more mafia-related problems.

Amanda is still living on the island, stuck in a rut, when trouble crosses her path again. Curious, and looking for a distraction from her break-up with her boyfriend Rupert, Amanda ends up spending some time getting to know the island's handsome new visitor...

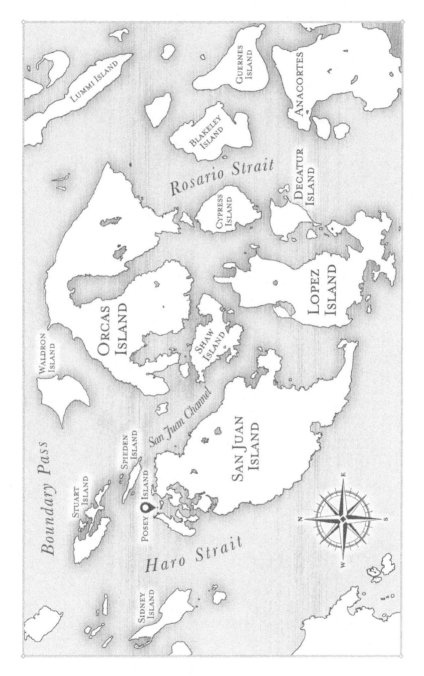

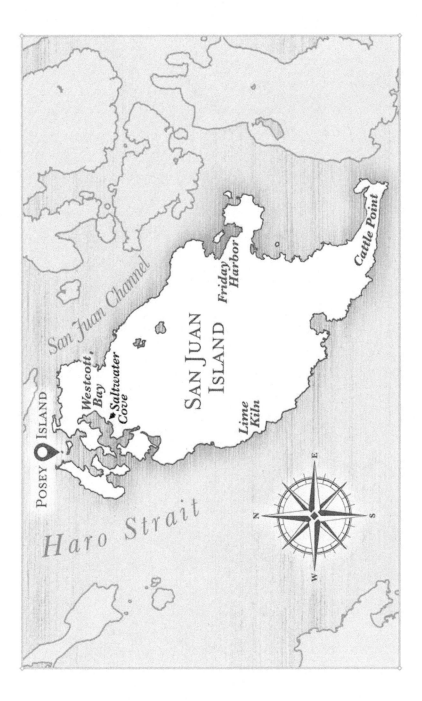

Chapter 1

It was the puddle that sealed it for her.

Amanda was able to grin and bear everything up until that point. She could handle being called into the Seattle office on short notice. It was for an important meeting, after all, and she was able to get in quickly by using her last seaplane ticket.

She'd bought a ten pack of flights on sale weeks ago, never thinking she'd need to fly between Friday Harbor and Seattle urgently so many times, but oh well. That was life with Erica as a boss, a woman who was *convinced* that the smallest missteps at their mid-sized marketing firm were of life-or-death importance.

She didn't complain when Erica subsequently called her out of that important meeting to throw a scrap of paper at her and mutter, "I need lunch on my desk by 12:30." (There was no "please" or "thank you" involved. Just a bright pink Post-it note with a scrawled message: "Carpy's Cafe – Caprese sandwich with chips. Don't let them put soggy tomatoes on it this time.")

The rain on her walk to the cafe didn't bother her – not truly, since she'd remembered to bring her umbrella and her hair was already irredeemably frizzy. Though the first quarter mile of the trip in the downpour rendered her cute flats completely soggy, it was fine. At least she was getting some exercise.

Amanda managed to keep her cool through all of it. She held her head high and didn't allow the absurd little frustrations to get her down. Until, that is, one of the frustrations jumped up and hit her in the face.

She didn't even see it coming; her vision was obscured by the umbrella. She didn't notice that a car swerved, jerking at precisely the right moment, to synchronize its passing with her hurried steps. She didn't see the water, arching with spectacular grace and accuracy, before it hit her in the chest, splattered onto her face and soaked into her clothes.

It was that moment, when the malicious tsunami puddle made contact, that it all came crashing down.

Amanda stopped in the middle of the sidewalk and screamed.

The rain continued, unmoved by her rage. She took a deep breath and closed her eyes; she could feel the water dripping off of her clothes. She raised a hand to her face, picking cinders off of her skin.

Amanda looked around to see that the car was gone and that no one was paying her any attention. That was one of the benefits of being in a big city – no one cared to notice her losing her temper. Or her mind.

The downside, though, of being in a big city was that someone embraced that same anonymity to splash her in the first place.

She now felt slightly embarrassed by her scream. It was the wrong way to react – she knew that. But she'd just snapped.

Amanda readjusted, moving her umbrella to her other hand, and whispered to herself that she just needed to regain her composure and get through the day. There was still almost half a mile before she'd get to Erica's favorite sandwich shop, and there was no point in storming around in a fury. She repeated it to herself three times before she calmed down.

After wiping her face with the sleeve of her jacket and taking another deep breath, she looked up and saw a deli across the street.

NYC Bistro Deli. It looked like a *perfectly* good deli. It was like an omen, smiling down at her. Were the clouds parting? Was the rain slowing down?

Amanda shifted and her shoes let out a squeak. Would Erica know the difference?

Probably.

At this point, did Amanda care?

No.

No she did not.

She hurried across the street and ran inside the shop, grateful for the refuge from the rain. Using a handful of napkins, she dried off as well as she could. When she caught her reflection in the front window, she didn't look *great,* but it wasn't as bad as she'd imagined.

Sure, her hair was a wild, humid mass hovering around her head, but the makeup she'd put on that morning was still holding strong. Her mascara had run a tad, but she was able to fix it with a napkin, too.

After throwing the glob of napkins into the trash, Amanda took a spot at the end of the line. There were only two people ahead of her – a guy who'd just stepped up to be helped, and an older lady with perfectly coiffed hair. She had a plastic sort of bib on her head – like a hair rain jacket. Maybe that was what Amanda needed – just to encase herself in plastic every time she was sent out on an errand.

She smiled – she wasn't against the idea, but she wouldn't even know where to buy such a thing. She stood there, studying the back of the woman's head, when a man walked over, first looking at the display of potato chips nearby, before parking himself in front of the older lady.

The lady let out a loud sigh and turned around, as though looking for an ally. Amanda shook her head in disgust.

The guy took no notice of their quiet protests.

She could feel the anger building in her chest. It was always harder for her to control her temper after losing it once; it was like she had a loose grip of it for the rest of the day.

She stared knives into the back of the man's head as the grasp on her temper slipped through her cold, grimy hands. Amanda took two steps forward and tapped the man on the shoulder.

He turned around, shooting a perturbed glance down at her.

"Uh – yes?"

"Hi – there's actually a line." She flashed a smile. "It starts behind me."

He jerked his shoulder away and turned back around.

Amanda and the lady locked eyes. It seemed that woman was just as angry as Amanda, her mouth hanging open and her eyes narrowed. She nodded, and Amanda nodded back before stepping in front of the man. "Excuse me, you just cut in front of both of us."

"What's your problem?"

"I just told you." Amanda said, staring at him. "I just watched you cut in front of me and this very nice lady here, and *that's* my problem."

The woman behind the deli counter called out, "Next!"

The man took a step forward, but Amanda wouldn't budge. She squared her shoulders and crossed her arms, moving in front of him. "I'm sorry, do you not understand how lines work? That lady is next."

"If you – "

Amanda ignored him and turned to the woman. "Go ahead, ma'am, you were next."

The woman smiled and slowly walked toward the counter. Amanda maintained eye contact with the guy, saying nothing else. After staring at him for half a minute, he let out a huff and walked out of the restaurant.

Amanda smiled to herself and got back in line. There was nothing that she hated more than a bully.

Well...that wasn't true. There was nothing she hated more than a bully that she *couldn't* stand up to.

Guy in a sandwich shop? Sure, no problem!

Person who sent her *to* the sandwich shop?

Not a peep.

She stepped up to the counter and placed an order for a caprese sandwich. Amanda was debating the health of the tomatoes when she thought that she heard a familiar voice.

She turned around to see where it was coming from. There was a table near the entrance, up against the large windows. Two guys were sitting there – one she definitely didn't recognize, and the other had his back turned to her.

She turned around to see that the tomatoes, for better or worse, had already found their way onto the sandwich. Erica would have to deal with it.

Amanda placed an order for a coffee for herself and made sure to pay separately – though Erica always asked for a receipt, she hadn't gotten around to paying Amanda back in months.

It was usually no more than ten dollars here or there – coffees, lunches and sometimes snacks. Amanda felt petty even bringing it up to her boss, but at this point, Erica's tab was nearing a hundred dollars!

It was starting to get annoying, especially because Amanda specifically packed her lunch so that she could save money and time when she had to work in the office.

After paying, she stuffed the receipt into her pocket and was almost to the door when the familiar voice rang out again.

"Let me tell you, we're *very* excited about this opportunity."

She stopped. Who *was* that? Why did he sound so...

Amanda froze. He sounded familiar because he *was* familiar. It was the voice of the man that she'd tasered only a few short months ago – Lenny!

Why wasn't she wearing a scarf or something to hide her face? She stepped to the side, standing at the sugar and milk counter and slowly removing the lid from her coffee.

She turned to get another peek. Though she still couldn't see his face because his back was to her, the outfit was there – the tracksuit. Oh my goodness – *why* was it always a track suit?

He was talking to a younger guy, probably in his twenties, who was professionally dressed in a gray suit.

Amanda picked up a packet of sweetener, pretending to study it as she listened in.

"And I can't tell you how excited we are to have you," the younger guy said. "At DGG, we've got the talent of a big group with the personal touch you'd find at a small firm."

Was this guy a lawyer or something? Lenny probably needed a lot of lawyers...

Amanda pulled out her phone and Googled "DGG Seattle."

All of the results were for a company called Dirk Gold Group – an investment firm.

A deli employee walked past Amanda and set a cup of coffee down in front of Lenny.

"Thank you Miss," he said.

In her peripheral vision, Amanda could see that his eyes lingered on the poor woman long after she walked away.

Ew.

Same old Lenny.

He turned back. "You know what Will, that's what I really like to hear. And I like you. I really do."

"That's great, because we like you too!"

Lenny chuckled. "I'm going to grab some milk for my coffee, one second."

Shoot!

She couldn't let Lenny see her. Amanda spun, grabbing her coffee and using the sandwich bag to hide her face as she moved toward the door.

"Please, let me get it for you," the other guy said, quickly standing up.

Amanda, still hiding behind the bag, didn't see the guy and didn't slow her panicked escape. Their bodies collided and the flimsy cardboard cup didn't stand a chance; the cup exploded between them, sending coffee all over Amanda's already damp shirt and splashing onto the man.

"Wow, I am *so* sorry – " he started to say before Amanda cut him off.

"It's fine, sorry, got to run!" she yelled, pushing the door open and rushing out before anyone else had a chance to see her.

Chapter 2

The last time that Will had gone to the San Juan Islands was when he was a kid. His parents had taken them there for an overnight camping trip. They weren't able to take vacations when he was growing up, so at the time, he thought the camping trip was the coolest thing they'd ever done.

He didn't know that his parents had to do everything on a shoestring budget, and that they didn't pick camping because they were outdoorsy – rather because it was as close to free as it could be, with the borrowed tent they'd gotten from a friend at church.

Will hadn't known the difference – he had a great time and came back to school to tell everyone about how much fun it was to sleep under the stars and skip rocks across the chilly waters. One of his schoolmates, Ellison, quickly put him into his place, telling him, "Camping is for poor people. That's what my dad says."

After that, Will didn't talk about the San Juan Islands anymore.

But it was a new day and he was a new person. When he drove onto the ferry and parked his car, he felt like he was on an adventure. He didn't care what the Ellisons of the world said anymore. He was making his own way, and somehow it felt right that the first steps were on San Juan Island.

His new assignment was to manage, maintain and repair properties on the island for Dirk Gold Group and their clients.

"If you can cinch this," his boss Gordon told him, "I see a junior partner position in your future."

That was music to Will's ears. He would do whatever it took.

He wasn't sure why, but everything about the ferry delighted him. Perhaps it was because in his memory, the ferry seemed like a magical place. Even now as an adult, it felt that way.

He climbed up the narrow stairs from the bottom deck and walked the distance of the decks three times. He went out front and peered over the railing, then out back to look at the wake. He loved the feeling of the wind against his face, and he loved the coziness of stepping back into the cabin where people were playing games, chatting and enjoying snacks.

Maybe it was childish, but he was giddy from it all. The San Juan project could solidify his position in the company for good, *and* he was getting to spend time in a beautiful place.

After getting coffee, he decided to walk around the ship one more time, just to observe all of the people and admire the views from different windows. He was halfway through this trip around when he saw someone who looked familiar. It took a moment to place her, but he was pretty sure that she was the woman from the deli – the one who had slammed into him with a coffee and then run off!

"Excuse me?" he said, stepping toward her.

She didn't look up from her laptop, seemingly engrossed in her work.

"Excuse me, Miss?"

She glanced at him. "Can I help you?"

"Don't I know you from somewhere?"

She looked back down at her screen. "Probably not."

He smiled. "No, I think I do."

This time she stopped typing and actually looked at him.

He pulled open his suit jacket to reveal the coffee stain that covered half of his once-white shirt. "NYC Bistro Deli?"

"Oh. Yeah – that does ring a bell."

"I *thought* it was you," he said, taking a seat across from her. "It's nice to see you again."

She looked him up and down. "Did you follow me all the way here? Just because I spilled some coffee on you?"

"No!" He sat back. "Not at all – I have some business on San Juan Island."

"Sure. Stalker," she muttered, looking back at her screen.

Will couldn't help it – he laughed out loud. She was so delightfully disdainful. "I swear that I'm not a stalker. I work at DGG – er, Dirk Gold Group. We own some properties on San Juan Island, and I was put in charge of them. That's it. I swear."

She sat back and crossed her arms. "Do you have a card or something?"

He nodded, eagerly reaching into his pocket and handing her his business card.

"Will Harrington?" She set the card down in front of her. "I'm Amanda."

"Nice to meet you Amanda."

"So...why San Juan Island?"

He shrugged. "Lots of reasons, really. There are a ton of vacation homes here that need to be managed, and some of the owners like to make a little profit on the side by renting their properties out in the off-season. So I manage a lot of those – or, well, I'm *going* to manage those."

"I see."

"It's more than that, though. We're an investment group, but for real estate – what they call a REIT, or real estate investment trust. So, say that you'd like to get involved in real estate investment, but you don't have time to manage a property, or to deal with buying and selling. You can work with our group, and it's sort of like investing your money in an index fund. But instead of stocks, it's a bunch of properties that we manage."

"I know what a REIT is," she said flatly.

"I'm sorry," he laughed again. He felt like he was on trial in front of this woman. "I didn't mean to over-explain to you. I've been working with the company for a few years, and no one ever really seems to understand what I do there, so it's a habit."

She nodded. "Okay."

"I actually have a lot more experience on the building side of things," he found himself saying. Though she was hinting that she wanted him to be quiet, he couldn't stop talking. "My dad was a contractor – well, he still is, but he can't really work anymore. He injured his back. But I spent a lot of years working with him and understanding what goes into maintaining a property, so I'll be handling that as well."

She eyed him for a moment and he felt the urge to speak again, but resisted this time. He realized that he was talking *far* too much. Amanda was quite pretty – which was part of the reason he felt so tempted to talk to her. She probably had guys hitting on her all the time, though. And it seemed like she was more than adept in warding them off.

"Have you ever been to San Juan Island before?" she asked.

He shook his head. "Not recently. I went camping here with my family when I was a kid. I'm excited to be back. Have you ever been before? From what I remember, it's gorgeous."

"Yes, it's beautiful," she said. "I grew up here."

"No kidding! I get the feeling that it's a very small town kind of place. Everyone knows everyone, sort of thing."

She nodded. "It is."

"So maybe..."

He paused. He wasn't winning any points with Amanda, and she obviously wanted him to go away.

Yet her contempt only interested him more. He might as well give it one last shot – he had nothing to lose.

"You owe me some introductions after covering me in coffee."

She laughed.

Ha! She *actually* laughed.

Maybe he had a chance after all?

Chapter 3

This guy wasn't going to give up easily, was he?

At first, Amanda was startled when she saw him. She thought he'd followed her to the ferry and that Lenny might not be far behind.

But the more that he talked to her (rather, talked *at* her), the more she realized that this guy was on his own, and that Lenny would probably never want to return to San Juan Island to face her (or her dad) again.

Margie had upgraded Amanda's purse to have a reasonably sized can of pepper spray. She casually reached over to her purse to make sure it was still there.

"Really? You think that I owe you something?"

He flashed a smile – a charmer, for sure.

"I'd prefer an introduction to the island and its people," he said. "But I'd settle for a single dry cleaned shirt."

"A dry cleaner, eh?" Amanda crossed her arms. "There aren't any dry cleaners on San Juan Island."

"Really? See, this is the kind of expertise that I need. From an authority on rural island living."

"I'm just pulling your leg," she said. What kind of bumpkins did Will think lived on San Juan? Or was he just gullible?

"Ah. Of course."

"I could introduce you to some of the other services that we simple country folk have on the island. The schoolhouse. The saloon. The...sheriff's department."

He smiled, leaning in. "How kind of you to welcome an outsider like me directly into the sheriff's department."

"Yes, the official welcome center for stalkers." She cracked a smile. "On second thought, what if the people of San Juan Island don't look favorably on companies that try to invade and take over their homes to turn a profit?"

He clasped his hands together on the table between them. "Then that's good for me to know, too. Important for business."

She had to resist the urge to scoff. Did he *really* think that she'd want to help him? "You're all business, then? Tell me, Will – why did you go into finance?"

Without missing a beat, he replied, "For the money, of course."

She laughed. "Fair enough. At least you're honest about it."

"Anyone who says anything different is a liar. But obviously, it's more complicated than that. And I think there can be a balance."

"You mean a work-life balance?" Amanda didn't need another guy in a suit lecturing her on work-life balance. Last month, they had a work meeting scheduled from six until eight in the evening to talk about work-life balance. The irony of staying so late to discuss the importance of free time escaped management.

"No," he shook his head. "Work-life balance doesn't exist. I'm talking about a balance between our company making money and preserving the quaint charm of a community."

"That's one thing we can agree on."

He raised an eyebrow. "The importance of preserving quaintness in an ever-changing world?"

"Well, yeah, that too. But greed is a surefire way to destroy any sort of wholesomeness."

"Right." He nodded. "It's not in our best interest to turn the island into the next Vegas."

That wasn't much of a comfort. "Sure. But I meant about work-life balance being a lie. You're right. Even the phrase makes me sick. *Work-life.*" She scoffed. "As though it should be fifty-fifty. Here's work, that's one of the halves – and the other half is everything else in your life: family, friends, going to the library, baking...as though the goal is to make work half of your life."

He smiled. "You're right. Though the goal of work is, of course, to absorb as much of your life as it can. For me, work is about being able to create your own freedom. And that's why I like finance – with the right skills and hard work, I can actually make some money."

"Money to buy back your freedom?"

He smiled. "Sure. Time *is* money, after all."

Oh great. Another money-obsessed wannabe mogul coming to the island. Amanda couldn't think of anything the island needed *less* than another greedy guy with big ideas.

Yet here he was, sailing over to pillage whatever he could – and apparently, he was also working on Lenny's behalf. Did Will even know what kind of people he was working with?

If she told him, would he care?

Amanda had no idea. But if Lenny was making a move, she wanted to know everything about it.

"Well...I guess I could show you around a bit," she said.

"Really?" He crossed his arms. "Even though you don't approve of my company 'invading' and turning a profit? That seems...generous."

Shoot. He was suspicious of her. And reasonably so – Amanda's surly demeanor was best used to scare people off, not to pull them into a scheme. Schemes were Morgan's territory.

Amanda had rarely tried turning her attitude around. Her mom had always told her, "You'll get more flies with honey than you will with vinegar." But it didn't matter how often she heard it; all Amanda had was vinegar

"Well, in exchange..." She cleared her throat. "Maybe you can help me with my house."

"Your house?"

It was best to go with a half-truth. "Yeah, I own a place on the island, but I work in Seattle. I've been working remotely a lot, though I don't think that it's a long-term solution."

"I see. So you might be looking to sell?"

Amanda tried to block the image of her father's disapproving face from her mind. If he knew that she was pretending to put their house – no, *his* house – on the market...she might end up getting it worse than Lenny. "I might be. Or maybe I could rent it, when I'm not here? Like you mentioned."

"Ah," he uncrossed his arms, "so you're not completely hostile to DGG, then."

Amanda looked back at her computer screen, determined to look indifferent. Though he might be money obsessed, Will didn't appear to be dumb. If she wanted to get any information out of him, she'd have to play along. And convincingly. "I guess not."

"Well, my number is on my card, but let me give you my personal cell." He pulled a pen from his suit jacket and reached across the table.

Amanda caught site of an expensive-looking watch on his wrist as he wrote down his number.

"You can call me anytime."

What a smooth move!

If only Amanda had the capacity to be impressed. "Twenty-four hours a day?"

"Like I said – time is money."

Amanda nodded and slipped the card into her purse. "Cool. It looks like I'll be talking to you soon."

He took the hint – *finally* – and got up. He offered a handshake and Amanda accepted it. "Nice seeing you again, Amanda."

"You too, Will."

Once he was out of sight, Amanda pulled out her phone and texted Morgan. "More news on the deli front. I think I might have a lead."

Morgan answered moments later. "Cannot wait to hear! I'm headed home from a client meeting. See you there?"

"I'll bring coffee!"

After Amanda had spilled her coffee at lunch, it felt like the entire day had been a drag. It would be nice to get her caffeine fix – though now she felt oddly energized.

Morgan was already waiting in the living room when she got home.

"Is Jade here?" Amanda asked in a low voice.

Morgan shook her head. "We're in the clear. Talk!"

Amanda handed her a coffee and settled on the couch, telling Morgan all about the run in at the deli and meeting Will on the ferry.

"I really appreciate the dramatic retelling of the coffee incident in person," Morgan said. "I mean, it was funny through text, but just seeing you look like this." She waved a hand in front of Amanda. "And hearing the whole thing really adds to it."

Amanda laughed. "Yeah, whatever. I had a rough day. But listen – this next part is important."

She told Morgan about Will, his business and the lie she told him about her dad's house.

"Okay, so first of all, are you sure that Will isn't like...*close* with Lenny?"

Amanda shrugged. "Pretty sure. It was obvious that when they met in the deli, Lenny was meeting him for the first time. And he was all business."

"Who does business in a deli?" Morgan mused.

The mob. But Amanda couldn't tell Morgan that. "Will, apparently."

"We'd better look him up online just to be safe."

Morgan pulled out her phone and searched for Will Harrington. She easily found his entry on the DGG company website, as well as a personal account where he had posted some pictures – they were mostly from what looked like work events.

"Oh, he's *cute*!" said Morgan. "Are you sure that you only wanted to talk to him because of Lenny, or were you just looking for a reason to see him again?"

"Absolutely not. I don't find men who work with people like Lenny attractive."

"Are you sure?" Morgan zoomed in on a picture. "Look at him in this tuxedo! Hubba hubba!"

"Ugh, gross. Don't be fooled by a tuxedo, Morgan. He was quite proud of being a money-hungry, morally apathetic, finance-centric leach."

"Them's fightin' words!" Morgan said with a giggle. "Tiffany used to work in finance, didn't she?"

"She's different." Amanda paused. How could she explain how she felt about this? It wasn't like *all* finance people were bad. It was just...him. Or anyone who would work with Lenny. "It *is* a fight! He probably wants to turn the entire island into a big hotel. He doesn't care about San Juan. Look who he's working with!"

"I'm not arguing with you," said Morgan. "But you at least have to admit that he's cute."

"I will not."

"Come on."

"No! He's not cute."

"He is. He's a cutie."

"Not to me." Amanda said simply, standing up to toss her coffee cup into the trash.

"All right, so what's our next move? Are you going to tell your dad that you saw Lenny?"

"I don't know," said Amanda with a sigh. She felt guilty that she couldn't tell Morgan the truth about Lenny – that he actually *was* in the mob, and Margie's brother Mike was supposed to be keeping an eye on him through the FBI. Oh, *and* that she was sworn to secrecy.

Maybe she would reach out to Mike herself? Just to let him know that she was on to something?

But she didn't have any contact information for him. She'd have to ask Connor and then...

"I bet your dad would love to know that Lenny is messing around on the island again."

"Yeah, you're right. I could tell him, but I'm sure that he'll tell me to stay out of it. And he *really* won't like that I'm pretending to sell his house."

"Yeah, those are all good points." Morgan frowned. "Maybe you shouldn't tell him."

"At least not for now. Maybe when I have some more information?"

Morgan nodded. "Yeah. That makes sense."

"So, what should I do? Should I text Will and offer up my help?"

"Yeah, I think so. If he doesn't know anything, it'll just be a dead-end."

"Yeah. What's the worst that could happen?"

Morgan groaned. "Don't say stuff like that. You're going to jinx it."

"Oh Morgan – I'm pretty sure that we're all already jinxed. Or cursed, maybe."

She laughed. "Yeah. Maybe."

Morgan was being superstitious, but Amanda didn't believe in stuff like that. She texted Connor to get Mike's information, and then sent a second text to Will, asking when he would be free next.

No – Amanda wasn't going to be swayed by superstition. If she wanted something, she would go and get it for herself.

Chapter 4

Once Amanda was back in her room, Morgan decided to make her move. If she waited any longer, Connor might be tipped off and Teresa might be, too.

Morgan *knew* that there was something they weren't telling her about Lenny. Why did everyone act like it was totally normal and no big deal that a guy broke into Margie's house *with a gun?* Why did they all act like it was a silly misunderstanding? And how was it that Amanda just happened to be ready to taser him?

No one was talking, but Morgan was determined to figure it out.

She went to her bedroom and pulled out her phone to call Luke. He'd been in Vancouver for the last six weeks working on a film that Teresa helped him get involved with.

Luckily, January wasn't a big month for them as far as weddings go, so Morgan was able to handle everything on her own. She did miss him, though, even more than she expected to. Maybe that's why she was looking for trouble?

No, that wasn't it. Morgan was always looking for trouble.

He answered her call on the third ring. "Hello beautiful."

"Hi Luke," she said, smiling to herself. "How are things?"

"Oh you know, not bad. We're dealing with the tricky bit of editing, but Teresa is helping us out."

"Oh, is she?" Morgan tried to keep her tone casual. "I actually wanted to ask her a question."

"Hang on, I'll grab her. Is everything okay?"

"Yeah, everything's fine. Uh...well, you can't tell Jade. Or Connor."

"Oh, there's a secret?"

"Sort of. Amanda saw Lenny today in Seattle. And it's a long story – but I *still* feel like she knows more than she's letting on. And I just..."

Luke laughed. He was well aware of her suspicions. "All right, all right. Teresa is just walking by – I'll get her."

Morgan let out a sigh. She knew that her secrets would always be safe with Luke, even if he had no interest in partaking in the gossip with her. He'd been very focused in Vancouver, unlike she'd ever seen him before. It was now *she* who felt bored and stagnant.

"Hi Morgan! What's up?"

"Hey Teresa! So, this is kind of awkward..."

"What's wrong?"

"Nothing's wrong. I just had a question for you. Is Connor around?"

"He's not, but I can – "

"No, that's fine." Better even. Connor shut down gossip faster than anyone she knew. "Because I feel like he wouldn't want you to tell me. You know how he is."

Teresa laughed. "Why do I feel like I'm going to get in trouble?"

"You're not going to get in trouble. But let's say that maybe I, or someone else, thought they saw Lenny in Seattle?"

"Oh?"

"And maybe I – or that person – just wanted to know if Lenny has any other known associates that we should be on the lookout for?"

"I'm sure that Chief Hank would know better than I would."

"He's kind of a grump." Morgan smiled to herself. Understatement of the year. "And I meant more like people you knew from your days on set with him."

"Oh man, I don't know. Connor used to see him hanging out with a few guys at the resort. There was another guy who was always on set with him, but I never caught his name. I probably couldn't pick him out of a crowd if you paid me."

Morgan frowned. "Ah, okay. Have you heard from Chet recently?"

"Nope, can't say that I have. I'm sure he's planning some sort of a comeback, though."

Morgan laughed. "Can't keep him down for long. Well – thanks anyway. And thanks again for helping Luke! He's having the time of his life."

"It's been great having him here."

"That's good. Because despite what he might tell you, I *do* miss him.

"Oh wait, actually, I have heard a little bit about Chet."

"Yeah?"

"Well not about him, exactly. But his dad – John Benzini?"

Morgan pulled her laptop in front of her and typed his name into a search. "Did he work on the movie too?"

"No. It's kind of weird, I picked him up from the airport once. I thought he was involved with the movie somehow, but he never was. Not that I saw. He was super nice."

"Is he a director or something?"

"No. He's not involved in movies at all. He popped up kind of randomly, actually. There was this story about people being held at the US-Canadian border for hours when trying to travel. And I was worried that we might get stuck there sometime when we were driving through."

"Oh that would stink."

"Yeah, it hasn't happened but you know, I try to leave time for it. But anyway, I saw this news story with a senator who was promising to help anyone who had issues there, so I wrote his name down, but the weird thing was that on the news I saw him with Mr. Benzini!"

Morgan frowned. "So Chet's dad is a politician?"

"No, he's like a consultant or something. I guess it makes sense. It must've made him really wealthy, because Chet had expensive tastes."

"Yeah, that's for sure."

"Sorry I can't be of more help – but I have to run. Here's Luke!"

She talked to Luke for another half hour before he had to go, too. He was supposed to stay in Vancouver for another few weeks. Morgan felt like she might lose her mind before then, but she kept that to herself.

At least now she had something to occupy her thoughts. Morgan did feel bad that she bugged Teresa about Lenny. Clearly she didn't know anything, other than the fact that Chet came from a rich family. That was hardly a shock; the guy had his head permanently in the clouds.

The next day, Morgan had plans to get lunch with Margie and Jade. Even though she was busy with work, Morgan made an extra effort to plan social activities now that Luke was gone.

When they got into the car, Morgan told Jade about Amanda's run-in with Lenny and their new scheme.

Predictably, Jade didn't approve, immediately stating, "I don't like this."

"I know, but don't you think it's weird that Lenny is working with a company to buy properties on the island?"

Jade shrugged. "Maybe. Maybe not. What if he just decided it was a good investment opportunity?"

Morgan scoffed. "Oh come on, you have to realize that there's more to Lenny than they're telling us."

"I don't know anything, I've already told you. And if I did – I wouldn't tell you anyway!"

"Come on now, that's not true." Morgan studied her for a moment, but Jade didn't flinch. "We have to work together."

"I've got way too much going on – between work and opening the park, I don't have the energy to start scheming with you."

Morgan sighed. "But what if Lenny really is involved with the mob? What if – "

"What if he *isn't?* He probably liked San Juan but is scared to death that Amanda will attack him again."

Morgan laughed. "He should be scared."

"Talk to Chief about it if you're so worried."

"How about I ask your mom today? Just to see if she wants to..."

Jade shook her head. "Don't. You know how she is. She'll tell you something that you're not supposed to know and then – "

"Aha! So you agree that there's something that we don't know!"

"I mean, maybe? I don't know – no, I don't think so."

Morgan decided to leave poor Jade out of it and focus her attention on Margie.

After they placed their orders for lunch, she set the stage. "I talked to Luke yesterday."

"Oh good! How's he doing?" asked Margie.

"He's good. I talked to Teresa, too." Morgan took a sip of her coffee. "I asked her if she'd seen anyone from the old zombie movie."

"Oh, is she still working with some of those people?" said Jade.

Morgan resisted glaring at her. Jade knew what she was doing – and she should stay out of it if she didn't want to be involved! "Yeah, some of them. She hasn't seen or heard from Chet since she left the island."

Margie chuckled. "Well that's good news. Maybe he's given up on his directing career."

"Maybe. I asked her if she's seen Lenny around."

Margie cocked her head to the side. "Lenny?"

"Yeah – you know. The guy that Amanda tased?"

"You're on a first name basis with him, are you?" Margie said with a smile.

"Well, yeah. Chief framed his mug shot and hung it up in our house. He's like our fourth roommate."

"Well I hope that Teresa hasn't seen him."

Morgan shook her head. "She hasn't."

She waited, watching as Margie placidly mixed sugar into her iced tea and tidied up the used napkins around the table.

Either Margie learned how to play it cool, or she really didn't know anything else.

Shoot.

"So I guess that's good. No Chet and no Lenny. The only person that Teresa saw was Chet's dad, but that was on the – "

"What was Mr. Benzini doing in Vancouver?" Margie said.

Morgan paused. She'd never mentioned his name. "Oh, he's not in Vancouver – she saw him on the news. With some politician who's helping people at the border?"

"Oh, how strange." Margie took a sip of her tea, but it was too late. Morgan spotted the pink flushing into her cheeks.

Well, well. It looked like Benzini was a lead after all.

Chapter 5

Their plans settled on lunch that Friday at a deli in town. It didn't escape Amanda that Will had suggested another deli; did he do all of his most important work in delis?

She told herself not to bring it up or tease him; she needed to focus on learning more about his business and on getting information out of him about Lenny. Professional, yet friendly. That was the goal.

But when she saw him sitting there in a casual navy blue button down shirt, her plan went out the window.

"Oh, so *this* deli wasn't fancy enough for you to wear your suit?" she said as she walked toward him.

He stood from his seat. "Unfortunately, no. You'll have to settle for spilling coffee on what I've got on now."

She suppressed a smile. She did feel bad about the coffee. "If you go to the cleaners in town, you can put it on my tab."

"We made a deal," he said, shaking his head. "Your island expertise *or* a cleaning bill. Not both."

"Ah, right."

"And I'm trying to embrace the aesthetic of the island. You know, get to know the place? Relax a little? Go tie-less. Unless you think I'm underdressed."

"No, you're fine. And you managed to pick the best deli on the island." She paused. No need to compliment him and give him a big head. "Do you do all of your business in delis?"

He laughed. "I guess so. What can I say? I'm a sucker for freshly baked bread."

"Did you already place your order?"

"No, I was waiting for you. And your recommendations."

She had probably, at one point or another, tried every sandwich that this place made. He didn't need to know that, though. They stepped up to the counter and after a bit of back and forth, both placed their orders.

After paying, they took their seats at one of the small tables.

"I have to say," he said as he settled in, "for being such a small island, there seem to be a lot of great restaurants and amenities."

Amenities. Is that how Will saw the world? A checklist of conveniences? "Yeah, it's not bad."

"You said that you grew up here? What was that like?"

Amanda was about to take a bite of her sandwich when she faltered. She was hit with a memory – it was one of her with her mom, sitting at the other side of this restaurant, eating meatball hoagies after a high school football game. Amanda vaguely remembered telling her mom about the boy that she liked, giggling manically. She couldn't remember what her mom said about him. It was starting to feel like she was forgetting her mom's voice...

"It was nice," she said. "Peaceful – idyllic, I guess. But you know, kind of boring."

"But you still enjoy living here?"

She nodded, taking a sip of her soda. "Yeah. I've been away for a few years, though. My job had me working in London, and I only just came back a few months ago."

"Couldn't stay away?"

What was the harm in telling him the truth? Amanda wouldn't be able to keep lies straight, and Will seemed harmless enough. "Not exactly. My dad and my stepmom got into an accident, and I came back to help them recover."

"Oh yikes, are they okay?"

She nodded. "Yeah, they're fine now. It took a few months for them to get back to normal, though. My dad is back at work. He's the Chief Deputy Sheriff."

Will smiled. "I think I'd like to get on his good side then."

"Good luck with that," she said with a laugh. "He's even less friendly than I am."

"And what about your mom? Does she still live here?"

Amanda set her sandwich down. "No. Well – she never wanted to leave."

"Oh. Does she live here part time, like you?"

Why was she being so awkward about this? "No. She passed away, actually."

"I'm sorry to hear that."

That's why she was being awkward. She didn't want to hear his condolences. She knew that he didn't mean them. How could he? How could he know what it was like to come back to this island, to see her everywhere and yet have the memory of her mom slipping through her fingers?

"It's okay. It's been a while." Another lie. Somehow time didn't seem to be helping much. She needed to change the subject. "I do think that most people who grew up here have a hard time leaving for good. I don't think that I appreciated the beauty of the island until I lived somewhere else, though."

"Yeah, I grew up in the eastern part of the state. Really small town, rural. It's very different over here."

"It is."

"Did you go to school locally?"

Why was he acting like he wanted to get to know her? All he cared about was her property. As he'd said, time is money. But he was good at pretending to be interested in her – a good salesman. "No, I'd wanted something different for school. I got a scholarship to Penn State, and spent my time on the East Coast."

"Ah. Nice. I think that being so well-traveled only makes you a better judge of what's valuable here on the island."

Valuable – what a word! She could only tell him what was valuable if they valued the same things. And they didn't! "Sure."

"I went to Washington State," he said. "To be honest, I've barely left Washington for most of my life. I did work in the New York City branch for a few years, and that was a big change."

She reminded herself that she needed to be somewhat friendly. "Oh, I bet. Living in London was a huge change for me as well."

"Do you miss it sometimes?"

What was with these questions? Of course she missed it. And at the same time, she didn't. Who was he to ask her this stuff?

Maybe she just missed her ex, Rupert? Or maybe she missed the bakeries where she could sit, undisturbed, compiling an album of pictures of her mom. That was what she did in the early days – she'd just linger, completely alone, but surrounded by people. And she'd tell Rupert all about her mom, the woman he'd never get to meet, and he'd say things like, "You're strong like her," or "I can see her in your smile."

It'd been eight weeks since she last tried to contact him, and he'd mostly blown her off. Her heart felt literally weighed down in her chest; it'd been months since they broke up. Would it ever get any easier?

"Yeah, there are things I miss."

"You're more generous than I am, then," he said. "There are a lot of cool things about New York City. Everyone knows that. All of the movies are made about New York – it's always with these people who fall in love with the city, and they say it becomes part of them and yadda yadda."

"And that didn't happen for you?"

"No. Not at all. I felt like a subway rat half the time. Like an *actual* six foot tall rat, dragging an entire pizza down the platform with its teeth."

Amanda laughed. "That is...horribly evocative."

"That was my level of desperation. It was my fault, though. I lived on Long Island and our office was in Manhattan. The commute wasn't terrible, but I worked all the time so...I probably didn't get as much out of it as I could've."

She nodded. Did he talk to all of his clients this way? No wonder Lenny liked him – he seemed down to earth. He was well practiced.

He kept talking. "The thing about New York City is that it's a really great time – *if* you have money. If you don't, well, get ready to drag a New York slice with your teeth."

Amanda almost choked on her soda. She didn't want to admit it, but rehearsed or not, the guy was funny.

"Plus, I always had a dog growing up, and I couldn't keep one in college, but I thought that once I had a job I could get one. But it's really hard to have a dog in New York City – have you ever been there?"

She nodded. "I have."

"There's not a ton of grass. That sounds stupid but it's a real problem. And again, if you work all the time...well, you need to hire a dog walker, and then you need a car because how do you get them anywhere?"

"And you need to not work all the time, so the dog recognizes you when you walk through the door."

"Right, and you have to be careful that the rats don't come after your dog and try to drag him into the sewers."

She laughed. "It sounds like you really don't like rats."

"I don't. It's no joke! Did you see that video making the rounds last week? A rat climbed onto a guy's face! He was sleeping on the subway, and it climbed *right* onto his face."

"Ew!"

He laughed. "I'm sorry, I never should've gone off on that tangent. Now you can tell me how much you love New York City and how much I've offended you."

She smiled. How much effort would it take for her to learn to talk to people like this, to try to be earnest? "No, you're fine. I can't say I've spent too much time there."

"That's a relief," he replied, taking a drink.

"So do you have a dog now?"

He shook his head. "No! That's the worst part. I can't have one in my place. And I'm still working all the time, now between here and Seattle. But at least sometimes I can go home now, see my parents and hang out with their dogs."

"There's a goal for you. Snag one of these island properties for yourself and start a dog park."

"Right," he said, mouth full of an overly large bite. "That's the dream."

"What do your parents do?"

"Well, my dad was a contractor. His business has really dwindled though, after his back injury. But we used to do all kinds of stuff – if you need anyone to hang drywall, pour cement, build stairs – I'm your guy."

She vaguely remembered him mentioning that but must not have fully believed him; she shot him a quizzical look. "Really?"

"Don't let the suit fool you," he said, taking another huge bite. "I have a lot of experience. But that's tough work. Back breaking."

She nodded.

"My mom was a librarian. Still is, actually."

"I see." Amanda realized that she was eating too fast – almost all of her sandwich was gone, and it was because she wasn't saying enough. She cleared her throat. "What kind of properties do you have right now?"

"I can show you. I've got a few from people who are looking to sell. I've got some rentals, and I've got a few fixer uppers." He pulled a folder out from his bag and slid it over. "Just to give you an idea of the caliber of properties we have. There's a wide range – everything from quaint little cabins to higher end stuff. We do it all."

She raised an eyebrow. "Are you insinuating that my house isn't high-end?"

He put his hands up. "No, no, I didn't mean that. I'm just saying – you know, you might hear the name and think – "

"I'm just kidding," she said, smiling as she flipped through the papers. "My house is nice but...you know, fairly modest. Nothing fancy, no ocean views."

"That's totally fine. You can see we've got some smaller homes – look at that one. That's a property that we just closed on; we're expecting to sell for about a hundred thousand more than the owner paid for it – after we do some improvements."

"What kind of improvements? Is this like house flipping – you'll paint the walls and put in some cheap floors and call it a day?"

He laughed. "No. My dad taught me the value of work well done. We're doing major changes here – redoing plumbing, new electric, opening up floor plans, and building additions to make the places more attractive."

She leafed through the pictures – it was true that some of these houses weren't so different than her house. Er – her dad's house.

"I have a theory that the people who want to rent homes for vacation are different than the ones who want to buy. Some of these places that we plan to rent are – well, see, what I'm thinking is that we'll add on a bedroom or two – nothing major, just enough that everyone can fit comfortably. You end up with a great property where people can vacation with their whole family, maybe even their extended family. And they come here, and have a really nice getaway without having to feel cramped or pay a fortune sticking everyone in a hotel."

She looked up at him, catching his eye. He paused and cracked what looked like a sheepish smile.

Was it sheepish? Had he gotten carried away? He was talking so quickly that it seemed like it.

Amanda smiled back at him. "That actually does sound like a good idea."

"Thank you." He cleared his throat. "And do you see that one there? If you just flip to the next page – those are the building plans we put together for that property. By finishing the basement, we're going to create a really great family space with a walkout into the backyard. And by breaking up that large bedroom into two different rooms, it becomes more comfortable for a group."

"I'm not going to lie – I don't know anything about building or improvements. But this all seems good."

"I hope so." He let out a sigh. "The trick is that we need to be careful with zoning. And I don't want to overcrowd neighborhoods or areas with these multifamily homes or rentals. We still want to have quality, single-family homes. Those attract a different sort of interest, and offer another reliable stream of income for the company."

Amanda finished her sandwich and bag of chips as Will told her about the plans for the various properties. Some of the places looked familiar – one was the previous home of an old middle school soccer friend. It made her feel a bit strange that a house she knew from childhood was going to be pulled into this scheme, but oh well. From Will's pictures, it looked like it had fallen into disrepair.

Will seemed knowledgeable about the big ideas. What he didn't understand were the island-specific challenges – the difficulty in getting building materials to the island, the challenges in booking contractors and companies, and which contractors to avoid entirely.

She debated whether she should help him with this, but ultimately she decided it was harmless. If it added to their relationship and made her seem like a more serious seller, all the better. It wasn't like these were guarded secrets of the island – she'd just been around so long that she knew all of it.

He took heed of everything that she told him, writing furiously on a notepad. By the time she got through everything, though, it was too late for her to show him her house. She needed to get back to work – and Jade would be back, too. No need getting Jade involved.

"Sorry that we went over," he said, shoving his notebook and folder back into his bag. "I really appreciate you taking the time to talk me through all of this."

"Sure. You're welcome. Maybe we can set up a time that I can show you my house?"

He nodded. "Absolutely."

She took a breath. She had to make some progress on the Lenny front. "And maybe you could show me some of these other properties? You know – just to get a feel for the market?"

"Of course, anything you like."

She smiled. Bingo. This might be all that she needed.

When Amanda got back home, she logged into her laptop to make sure that she wasn't in trouble for anything at work. Luckily, there were only three emails from her boss, and none of them were at a livid-level that demanded immediate response.

She pulled out her phone to text Morgan the update and saw that she had a message from Rupert.

Rupert!

"Hey Amanda, how are you? I've got some news – I'm not sure how to tell you this...but I'm working in the Seattle office and I was hoping I'd run into you soon?"

Her stomach dropped. She had *no* idea that he was going to transfer to the Seattle office! Did this mean that he'd missed her? Did it mean that they were going to get back together?

No, she shouldn't jump to conclusions. But there was a flutter in her chest. There must've been a reason why she couldn't forget him for all of these months. A reason she kept dreaming of him. There really still *was* something between them. She'd just been waiting for something – anything to confirm that feeling.

And here it was – a sign. Rupert had come to Seattle at last.

Chapter 6

She rushed off so quickly that Will didn't have a chance to set up another meeting with her.

Maybe he'd bored her to death and she was just trying to get away from him? He tried asking her about herself – he was dying to know more about her – but she was quite tight-lipped. He learned that she worked for an advertising agency, but she soon changed the subject.

It seemed like she was *somewhat* interested in the properties, and sensing that, he babbled on like a fool. What was he even talking about for so long?

And *what* was all that rat talk?

Will rubbed his face in his hands. She probably thought he was a moron.

Ugh. There was something about her. Whenever she was quiet or just staring at him, he felt the urge to fill the silence. He wanted to make her laugh, or at least keep her from walking away. It made him feel...desperate?

No, that wasn't the right word. It was more like he was trying on every hat in his repertoire to keep her attention.

Amanda was a tough nut to crack, and if she wanted to add her property to their portfolio, he would put in the work for it.

Though he had no idea if her property would be of use to the company, he could at least pretend that's what he was doing.

Yeah, that's what he could tell himself. That he just *really* wanted to add her property to his portfolio.

On her advice, he took some time to walk around Friday Harbor and get a feel for the place. There weren't many people out – it was a chilly day, and the clouds were threatening rain.

He peeked into the windows of the shops and studied the menus posted outside of the restaurants. He could see the charm of the place, both for vacationers and for buyers. Apparently, there was a big retired population on the island as well. He made a mental note to compile a list of community resources. Those were always good to put in descriptions, whether they were selling a property or renting it out.

He decided to get a cup of coffee at a café and take a seat outside overlooking the ferry terminal. A ferry was pulling up and Will was again struck by the enormity of the ships. He'd heard some people complaining about the ferry being late and he made another mental note to highlight the concept of "island time" in his listings. If he set the right expectations, people would react accordingly.

Despite the chill, he was content to sit at the cold metal table for the rest of the day, watching the comings and goings of the boats, and admiring the cycles of excitement and quiet when the ferries arrived and departed from the dock.

He wasn't that far from Seattle, but everything felt so different. Even the birds looked different. He wasn't a wildlife expert, but some of these birds looked completely foreign. There was one with an exceptionally long neck – was that a heron? Another, he could've sworn, had what looked like a blue mohawk of feathers atop its head. It flew off before he could take a picture. There were also a lot of fancy looking ducks – or were they not ducks? They were all swimming around, but probably not all birds that could swim were ducks...

Despite his bird-related knowledge being poor, Will felt like he could watch the birds bob and dive for hours. At some point, the sky even cleared out, filling with clean, white clouds so bright they were almost blinding against the brilliant blue sky.

When was the last time he'd stopped to look at the sky or at exotic birds? Maybe these were all regular birds, he didn't know.

But still. He rarely slowed down, yet San Juan was forcing him to look around. The appointments that he'd set up with people on the island – plumbers, contractors, zoning board members – were all delayed, much later than he'd like. But no one was in a rush to get his business, so all he could do now was wait and stare at birds.

Maybe DGG's ideas for these properties were silly to a native, and he was slowly going to have to piece that together on his own. But Amanda seemed to think that their ideas were at least interesting. Unless she was just being nice.

No, Amanda didn't seem like someone who would fake being nice. He appreciated that about her – there was no pretense. There was little of that sort of honesty in the business world.

He dealt with, and doled out, so much fake niceness that it made him sick; it made him feel hollow. Will knew that it wouldn't last forever; he wouldn't have to live this life indefinitely. He'd move up the chain and be able to act more normally.

Maybe that's why he'd tried so hard with Amanda. It was like she was the first real life form he'd encountered in years.

Sure, she had no qualms about making fun of him to his face. And she might've inherited her disposition from her frightening-sounding father. But she was different than any girl he'd met in New York City.

He didn't tell her about *that* part of living in the city – how he'd gone out to the clubs at his friends' urging, despite hating clubs more than anything.

But that was what his friends wanted to do, so he went. And they had to pay a cover charge, and then pay for a table, and pay for bottle service...it all added up. It was a waste of money to him, and even though the girls they'd meet looked like models – some of them actually *were* models – he had no interest in them.

And they had no interest in him. As soon as the free drinks ran out, they'd disappear, making sweet promises that they'd all "meet again."

Will didn't care – he gave them credit for figuring out a hustle. They had a game and they knew how to play it.

It was his friends that he thought were pathetic – believing they had a chance with those women, begging him to come along, to pitch in and pay for these ridiculous nights out. Will only agreed to go clubbing a handful of times before he put his foot down. While his friends had no qualms about pretending to be rich, it bothered Will quite a bit. It was not for him, and it was a silly way to waste money.

He had better things to do with his money. That reminded him, actually – he'd gotten a text from his mom during his lunch with Amanda. He pulled out his phone to see what it was about.

The message read, "Hey honey – it seems like there was a problem with the mortgage this month. Can you call me?"

He frowned. Why were there always problems when he tried to link to a new bank account?

He dialed his mom and she picked up right away.

"Hello?"

"Hey Mom, it's me."

"Oh good, I'm not bothering you, am I?"

"Not at all. What's going on with the mortgage?"

"I got a call today about it – oh, and a letter in the mail. Hang on, let me find it."

He waited as she shuffled around with papers.

"Okay here it is – it says that we're short four hundred and eighty dollars on the escrow? What's that about? Is this a scam?"

"Oh wait – that's my fault. I added on some insurance coverage and forgot to increase the payment."

"Coverage for what?"

"For wildfires. That'll cover a year. Trust me – it's worth it."

"Oh I don't want you to spend more money on things like – "

"I've run the numbers Mom, and believe me, this would save us money. It's not that much more per year. I'm happy to pay it. I'll top off the escrow today."

"Well..."

Clearly she was going to try to argue with him. He'd taken over their mortgage when his dad's back got worse. It wasn't even that expensive – much less than his apartment in New York City. What was actually expensive were his little sister's credit card bills. He needed to have a talk with her...

"Don't worry about it, Mom."

"Well, thank you. How's the island? Have you seen any whales?"

"Not yet," he said with a smile. "But I'll send pictures if I do?"

"That'd be nice."

His phone beeped – a client was calling. "Sorry Mom, I've got to run. Take care!"

"Okay, bye!"

He clicked over. "Hello, Will Harrington."

"Will, there's my guy! It's me, Lenny."

"Hey Lenny, how's it going?"

"Pretty good, pretty good. You know, I just wanted to tell you – we're still waiting on a few tenants to vacate our building, so maybe don't go poking around there until that's through."

"No problem. Just let me know when."

"Good man, I like that. Just stay away for now. All right, I'll let you know."

"Sounds good."

"Talk to you later."

Will didn't consider what he did as "poking around," but whatever. Lenny was the biggest client he'd ever gotten to work with, so he'd do whatever he was told.

Millionaires got their way – that was a rule – and not only did they get all the fake-niceness in the world, they also got their butts kissed the hardest. Even if Lenny was the associate and not the millionaire – Will wasn't exactly sure what his role was – he got the same treatment.

It was better, really, that he'd have more time to get things under control. He was much more interested in a certain client with a modest home, and an extensive working knowledge of the island and its charm...

Chapter 7

After her experience being caught in the downpour, Amanda had little interest in working in the office unless absolutely necessary. She initially debated telling Rupert that she was free for lunch any day, but decided to suggest that they instead change it to dinner so that she could avoid the office entirely.

Not wanting to sound too eager, she agreed to his suggestion for Thursday – though she wished it were sooner. She then spent the next few days fretting over every thought floating through her head.

Did he transfer to Seattle because he wanted to rekindle their relationship? Was he seeing someone else, or was he still in love with her? Was he having the same repeating dreams that she was having? Importantly, had she gained weight since he'd seen her last?

That was an awkward one. It'd been hard to stay active when she was wasting time driving to and from Seattle. Plus she'd never gotten around to renewing that gym membership...

Nothing she could do about it with such short notice, though. But why hadn't she thought to get a haircut in the last few months? It looked wild, haggard even.

She was able to rectify that, at least, by going in for a quick haircut on Monday. It ended up a little too short, but it looked cleaner.

The other problem was her wardrobe. She hadn't updated it *at all* since moving back to the US. Jade offered to let her borrow something, but Jade was much taller than she was – long and lean. Amanda was more...short and stout? She wasn't short, exactly; her dad just said that she was "compact."

He meant it as a compliment, because he was compact, too. She was always muscular, always stronger than the other girls growing up; it helped her in her soccer days. But it didn't help her feel feminine, and she struggled with it for years.

That was in the past, though. Mostly. She'd already wasted too much of her life trying, in vain, to look like someone else.

After her mom died, she realized how silly it all was – how little it all mattered. How could she waste so much precious time in her life worrying about something as meaningless as the shape of her body? It was something she had very little control over, besides losing a few pounds to be in the healthy range.

When she'd moved to London after her mom's passing, she began cautiously embracing her muscular build and wearing clothes that suited her better. Rupert liked her then, why shouldn't he like her again?

Luckily for her, Morgan, who was closer to her size, had a pile of new clothes that she was excited to share.

"Ooh, how about this sweater with this sparkly skirt?" she said, holding up the combination on herself.

Amanda frowned. "I don't think I want to do sparkly."

"True, no need to go big on the first date." She pulled out a bright pink top. "What about this? Too much?"

Amanda pulled the shirt on, studying herself in the mirror. "Is it supposed to be this tight?"

"Uh, I don't know, but I think it's working for you!"

Amanda laughed. "No, this won't be good. He'll be able to see my heart beating against my rib cage."

"Okay, fine. I have a dress? All black, might be a bit chilly but..." She dug around in her closet before finding it.

Amanda stared at it. It had long sleeves and looked like it'd hit her right at the knee. "This...could work for me!"

"Good. But after this, I need to take you shopping. No excuses."

Amanda laughed. "But I've been having so much fun wearing all of the clothes my boss hates."

"Hold up – what? You use your wardrobe to annoy your boss?"

She let out a sigh. "Yep."

Amanda knew it was a strange thing to do, but her boss Erica was a strange person. She tried to explain it to Morgan as best she could. Though not a fashionista, Amanda thought that she was pretty good at dressing herself at this point – but Erica disagreed.

Whenever Amanda was in the office, Erica would give her a quick up and down to check out her outfit. Sometimes she'd make a comment right away; other times, the rude comments would filter in throughout the day.

Amanda didn't mind the barbs – she was thick-skinned. She knew what she looked like. And she knew that it sometimes looked like she got dressed in the dark – because she was getting dressed in the dark!

Often, Erica would say something like, "Did Goodwill have a going out of business sale?" or "I didn't know that it was wear-your-grandma's-sweater-to-work day."

Amanda always laughed it off. It was actually amusing to hear how much her outfits bothered Erica; any time that she received one of these insults, she'd look at her outfit and make a mental note to wear it again.

The comments that *actually* annoyed her, and which she didn't tell Morgan about, were the ones that her boss made in front of clients. Last month, Erica ended a meeting with a client by saying, "And don't be worried about our company's style being as horrendous as Amanda's scarf, because it isn't!"

The client offered a blank smile, clearly unsure what they were supposed to do with that information. Amanda hated herself in these moments, but she laughed and brushed it off, just to get rid of the awkwardness.

What she *really* should've done was pull Erica aside and tell her that it was unprofessional to make fun of her in *any* way in front of clients.

But she didn't know how to do that, exactly.

"I have to be honest," Morgan said. "Your boss is a jerk."

"She's...complicated," Amanda replied, studying herself in the mirror. The dress was cute, but could she pull it off? Was this *the* outfit that Rupert would see her in for the first time in months?

"Doesn't sound complicated. It sounds mean."

"She thinks that she's my best friend."

"*What?* And that's how she thinks you treat friends?"

Amanda shrugged. "Well, yeah, I think so. She tells me all about her drama with her mom and her stepsister, and about issues she's having with her house and with her car. She'll call me to tell me this stuff and ask for my advice."

"You're just a good listener. And she probably doesn't have any real friends."

Amanda knew that was probably true; Erica spent all of her time working and seemed to have no social life. "Last year, she nominated me for the Five Star Award. Remember that?"

"Yeah, I remember when you came home that day. She threatened to fire you if you didn't come into the office for the day but wouldn't tell you why."

Oh yeah. That wasn't very nice. "Well, it's lame but it's the highest honor the company gives out – and I won it! When I went up to accept the award, I saw Erica in the crowd, tears streaming down her face."

Morgan studied her for a moment. "Weird."

"She was insanely proud. It's...a confusing relationship. And I do feel bad that she doesn't have any friends..."

"Sounds like a whole lot of not your problem," Morgan said with a laugh. "Well, whatever. She can't make fun of you in this dress. You look adorable! And wait – I have a necklace that'll go with it."

Amanda liked the necklace – she liked the whole look, which she finished off with a pair of boots. She felt as ready as she'd ever be for seeing Rupert.

Work kept her busy, along with some texts from Will planning another get together, until Thursday finally arrived. After she parked, she walked a short block and found Rupert standing outside of the restaurant in a familiar forest green jacket.

At least he didn't trouble himself with new clothes.

"Amanda, it's so good to see you." He pulled her in for a hug and she accepted, savoring the fleeting feeling of his arms wrapped around her. He smelled the same, his cologne transporting her back to London for a moment.

She pulled away from him, wishing that the hug could've lingered longer. The only person who hugged her nowadays was Margie. "Hey Rupert, it's so nice to see you."

"And it's so good to see you again. Oh, I already said that. Well," he laughed, jerking his head toward the restaurant. "I've got my name down for a table. Shall we?"

"Yeah, of course."

She told herself again and again not to be swept up, not to let herself get dizzy when she saw him. But when he opened the door for her, then followed her inside, it took all of her focus to avoid walking into something. She was walking in a daze and on a cloud.

He checked in with the hostess and they were led back to a table. Rupert offered to take her coat and she hesitated before unbuttoning it, revealing the simple black dress that Morgan helped her pick out.

"Thank you," she said as she handed off her coat to him.

He smiled at her. "You look – well, goodness, you look wonderful."

She smiled. She was glad that Morgan convinced her to wear the dress. "Thanks. You look pretty good yourself."

"Even with this?" He patted his belly and smiled. She'd missed that bashful smile. "Come now Amanda, don't tell me that your transfer here has turned you into a liar."

She laughed. "Not at all. You look nice."

Amanda took her seat, feeling somewhat proud that she was at least able to speak. She got tongue-tied so easily – though Rupert was never one to overwhelm her.

"I want to hear everything – how have you been? How's your dad?"

"He's good. Very good. I'm still living on the island, you know – with my sisters."

He groaned. "The dreaded stepsisters."

"No, it's not like that."

"You seem...different. Lighter."

"Do I?" Amanda picked up the menu, glancing over the appetizers. She wanted to pick something quickly – she'd foolishly not had a snack before she left the island, and now felt like she might faint. "I'm not sure what you mean."

"And I'm not sure what it is. Maybe this was just what you needed – to come home again. To make peace with everything."

"I don't know if I can say that *that's* what I've been doing."

"Right. Well, I'm sure that Erica is delighted to have you within her reach regardless."

"Oh boy, and how." She smiled at him. No need to bring up Erica. "But what brings you here? I had no idea you were transferring."

"They asked for volunteers to help with migrating to a new server. And when I saw that the opportunity was here in Seattle...I decided to take a chance."

"So it's temporary? The move?"

"It can be. Or I can stay. It's really up to me."

Interesting. Was he hinting that he'd changed his mind about moving or...was it just her wishful thinking?

The waitress arrived and they placed an order for drinks and an appetizer. Amanda asked Rupert about how things were going back in the London office, and he was happy to fill her in.

Her glass of wine arrived and as she listened, she drank it a bit too quickly; it was foolish, considering how hungry she was, and she could feel it soaking into her system. She felt relaxed. The nerves that tormented her all week were silent now.

It was just her and Rupert, like the old days. It felt like they had slipped right back to where they'd been before. And

Rupert was one of the few people who knew her history and really understood it. The first man she'd ever loved...

"Has it been hard?" he asked as he tore off a piece of bread.

"Ah – it's not been too bad. Erica is...herself. And the commute can be challenging, but I don't have to come in that often. It's been okay."

"I meant moving back to the island. I know that you've visited, but it's different living there, isn't it?"

She set her wine glass down. Yes, Rupert still knew her to the depths of her soul. "It has been hard, yeah. It's so strange to see San Juan Island moving on without my mother in it. When I lived in London, I could imagine that she was still there. I mean, obviously I knew she wasn't *there*, but sometimes it felt that way."

He nodded. "I know. It felt like you could pop back in and visit your old life."

"Right." She cleared her throat. "How about you? How are your parents?"

"Quite well. Nothing new. Mum has been pestering me to re-create some old family photos from when my brother and I were little. She saw something on the internet and got it into her head."

Amanda laughed. "You won't do it?"

"Eventually. Can't give the woman everything she wants. Maybe for her birthday."

Their meals arrived and Amanda stared at her plate. Somehow she was no longer hungry. Or perhaps it was easy to ignore when she focused on Rupert.

"You know, there's no other way to ask this. But are you seeing anyone?"

Amanda's eyes widened. She never in her wildest dreams would ask him a question like that, but she should have expected that he might ask her. "I'm not, no."

"I had to ask. I probably should've asked before I made the trip across the world, but here we are."

She laughed. "Yes, here we are. And you? Are you – ?"

He shook his head. "Nope. I'm hoping to spend some time here. Reconnect with old friends."

"What other old friends do you have in Seattle besides me?"

He smiled, shaking his head. "You've got me there."

Amanda laughed, covering her mouth with her hand. Same old Rupert. Always trying to say a thing without saying it. He was the most direct, indirect person that she knew. "Well, I hope that I can fill that role for you."

"I think you already have."

Her heart swelled. There was no need for him to spell it out, and no need for her to ask pushy questions. It seemed clear that Rupert had changed his mind about their relationship after all.

Chapter 8

The cake stared back at him from the conference room table, its white frosting stiff after being left out of the box for too long.

Balloons and sprinkles flanked the purple lettering, which oh-too-cheerfully spelled out, "Congratulations on Your Retirement Mike!"

Mike frowned. They'd insisted on getting him a cake, even though he told them that he didn't like cake.

That wasn't true, of course. He just didn't like *this* kind of cake. The frosting was too sweet; he could smell it from three feet away. It was too big and generic to be any good.

There was no *character* to this cake, it was simply a casualty of mass production. It was a cake abomination, nothing like the expertly crafted cakes he'd gotten used to in the endless five star bakeries of the city.

Sheet cakes, they called them. As if a *sheet* was a good way to measure cake. Suitable to feed a pack of children at a birthday party and also, apparently, a band of bored office workers.

There were paper plates stacked next to the cake, mostly leftovers from other events. The majority were birthday plates, but there was one stack proudly proclaiming "It's a boy!"

That, at least, made him laugh.

There was no use in avoiding this cake, or this party, any longer. As soon as people saw him walk into the conference room, they started to follow.

"Oh, it looks like you're finally ready to party!" said Cindy, one of the administrative assistants.

Mike didn't want to be rude. She clearly put some effort into putting all of this together for him. In fact, she'd probably put more thought into the entire thing than his boss did about his actual retirement.

"Thanks Cindy. This is great."

She smiled. "I'm sure everyone will be in soon – I'll send a reminder email. You can go ahead and start cutting pieces if you'd like!"

He smiled. "Sure."

At least cutting the cake gave him something to do. He got to work, placing the square slices onto plates and arranging them neatly on the table.

His old boss, Lincoln, walked in and made a face. "Vanilla? I knew they didn't like you, but come on."

Mike chuckled. "Thanks for stopping by. I'm told that the other side is chocolate."

"I'll take one of those, then. Don't tell my wife, she's been on me about eating too much sugar."

Mike cut into the other side of the cake; it was indeed chocolate. He cut Lincoln a big slice, and he accepted it with a wink.

Things had been much better under Lincoln, but it couldn't last. Lincoln was too good, and too smart – he was pulled into a special project and one of Mike's old coworkers got pushed into the supervisor position.

"Oh boy, is it too late for me to request extra balloons?"

Ned. There he was, as if on cue. Of course he was the sort of guy who would not-so-subtly demand extra sickeningly-sweet frosting.

"Hello Ned."

"Mike, you've done excellent work here, but since I'm still your boss for the rest of the day, you *have to* give me a cut of those balloons." He let out a nervous laugh.

Mike never understood what that was – that forced giggle that Ned had. It was like a tic or something, he did it all the time.

It had never bothered Mike before; he just assumed that the guy was sort of a nerd, not cut out for fieldwork. He was odd, a bit awkward, and a bit younger than Mike. At first he wasn't sure if Ned was just a product of his surroundings. Too much time on the computer, maybe? Mike didn't hold it against him, even though he was annoying at times.

They didn't see each other much, either. While Mike was building and supporting an undercover identity to befriend the Ukrainian mob, Ned was here, in the office, diligently working to kiss as many butts as he could.

He kissed butts all the way to the top.

"The balloons are yours," Mike said, handing him a plate.

Ned frowned. "Whoa man, this piece is huge!" Another laugh. "I could never finish it."

"Do your best." Mike turned back to the cake, hacking away, the lettering nearly broken up now.

After ten minutes of cutting, he could still make out the "Congratulations!"

Ha. As if his retirement was an achievement. Yes, there was a time that he was thinking about retiring, but that was before things started coming together. When Margie's house was broken into, it was like a missing piece of the puzzle jumped up and hit him in the face.

While he didn't like that it put his sister in danger, it also put everything into focus. Things started making sense. He was finally close to piecing it all together when Ned took over and hastily pulled him out of his post.

What was that all about? He still hadn't gotten any answers. Ned alleged that he'd gotten intel about Mike being in danger; he said that Mike needed to exit his undercover role immediately.

Mike never got a whiff of him being endangered, and he usually had a pulse on everything that was going on in that family. There still wasn't any clear indication that his life was any more at risk than usual.

But Ned didn't have to explain himself; Mike got pulled out with a slapped-together story that made little sense.

He shot a look over at Ned, who'd inserted himself into a conversation between some of the other office staff. His voice was loud and carried across the room. "Well, all I know is that when I'm the smartest person in the room, it's because I'm the *only* person in the room!"

His attempt at self-deprecation solicited a few fake smiles. They had no choice but to humor him; he was the boss, after all.

Mike rolled his eyes. He'd heard Ned say that phrase at least a dozen times. His false humility was one of the worst things about him, especially because despite what he said, his ego got in the way of all of his decisions. He was a power-hungry bureaucrat. Mike cursed himself for not noticing it sooner.

"Folks, gather around," Ned announced. "I wanted to say a few words about this wonderful public servant, Mike Grady."

Mike grimaced. There was nothing he could do to stop it.

"Mike joined the FBI twenty odd years ago, and back then, he was in the same shoes that many of you are in today."

Wrong. It was thirty-two years ago. He shot a look to Lincoln, who suppressed a smile.

"He worked his way up to be one of our finest agents. We're proud of the work you've done, Mike, and I'm excited to say that we have new agents here ready to step into your shoes. You're leaving your responsibilities in good hands."

It was almost like he'd ad-libbed a sendoff from a corporate handbook. "Thanks Ned."

There were a few claps before Lincoln stepped up to say something.

"I've known Mike since he walked into our humble office thirty-two years ago, fresh out of his Air Force career and looking for a fight. I was fresh out of the police force and as you can imagine, he found in me a partner to fight with."

Mike chuckled. "I had to toughen you up."

Everyone laughed, including Lincoln. "Well, it worked. We didn't always see eye to eye, but we always worked toward the same goal. My career and my life are better for having known you, and I know that everyone who's been lucky enough to work with you would say the same. It's been an honor serving with you, Mike. You'll be sorely missed."

Applause broke out again, much stronger this time. Mike smiled; he'd hoped to avoid sappiness. But coming from Lincoln, that was high praise.

Once the clapping died down, he cleared his throat. "Well, I guess I have to say something now."

More laughter.

He stood for a moment, everyone's eyes focused on him. What could he say that would mean something to all of these people?

He had an idea. Or at least, the beginning of one. "I was here the day that they installed one of our first computers. An office before computers, can you imagine? And now we've all got a computer in our pocket, or on our wrist." He paused; his goal wasn't to sound like an old man, but that was kind of how it was coming out.

He shifted his weight. "I watched the department go through changes – the same changes that we're watching happen across the rest of the world. We had to change, too, so we could keep up. Progress and change happen more and more rapidly now, and we have to be willing to meet it where it is.

"There will always be scummy people, trying to stay one step ahead of us. Sometimes it feels like we're chasing our tails, but you can't give in to despair. Keep changing. Keep progressing. You don't have to pretend to be the smartest guy in the room to make a difference."

Mike smiled to himself. Was Ned even sharp enough to catch that? Probably not. "I want to thank each and every one of you for the friendship and camaraderie that we've shared over the years. It's been a wild ride."

Applause broke out again, and almost instantly Ned raised his arms, motioning that they needed to quiet down. "All right, all right everyone. Don't forget that people are still working and we have to keep it down. Let's have some fun, but we report back to our desks in thirty minutes sharp, okay?"

Ever since Ned got the power to make people listen to him, he hadn't been able to contain himself. At least it wouldn't be Mike's problem anymore.

Since being hastily pulled in from his cover, Mike had a different set of problems. He had concerns for his safety and his family's safety.

When he was working under Lincoln, the plan was to remove him slowly, and to make it believable. But Ned was hasty, and the result was a botched story that had his close associates scratching their heads. Oh, and this ridiculous retirement party.

Mike didn't want a party. He wanted to uncover the connection between Benzini and the Sabini family. Sabini had been a thorn in Dmitry Koval's side for over fifteen years – long before Mike infiltrated the Koval family, posing as Gary Bomba.

Though the crime families dealt in a lot of the same business – drugs, illegal gambling, racketeering – somehow Sabini had pulled far ahead in recent years. It seemed like he had unlimited resources and Mike could never figure out why.

It was convenient, then, that Mike's retirement happened when he was so close to figuring it out. He didn't want to accuse Ned of being in Sabini's palm or anything, but something wasn't right. Something wasn't adding up.

Mike took a bite of cake.

Disgusting.

How many bites would he need to take so that no one was offended?

He took one more, then discreetly dumped his plate into the trash. He didn't have to worry about offending people for much longer – and he also couldn't count on help from the FBI anymore. He was on his own. And he didn't think it was a coincidence that Amanda contacted him last week, saying that she'd spotted Lenny in Seattle.

He was ready to follow up on that lead. As soon as this party was over, Mike was packing up what was left of his belongings and flying west.

Chapter 9

The next week was busy for Will. He finally got to meet with some contractors – the ones that Amanda recommended – as well as with a few suppliers. Amanda wasn't kidding when she said it would be tough to build on the island, but he was hopeful. He had a few allies now, and his boss said he could call in for extra help if needed.

He was trying to avoid that, if possible. Will would rather work sixteen hour days to get all of this done on his own. It wasn't that he was too proud to ask for help...

No, it was something else. There was pride involved, but it was more like he wanted to see if he could do it on his own. He was trying to prove something to his boss, yes, but even more, he needed to prove something to himself.

On Friday night, he decided that he deserved a bit of a break and that he should explore more of the island. He popped into the local brewery, hoping to snag a quiet table for himself, and was disappointed to find that the wait for a table was over an hour.

He was about to turn around and walk out when he spotted Amanda at the far end of the brewery. It felt like his heart skipped a beat. They'd been texting since their last meeting two weeks ago, but she hadn't offered to set a date to show him the house. It was hard to keep his mind off of her; he didn't even care about the house at this point. But he didn't want to come on too strong, either. And here she was, as if by magic.

He had to at least say hello.

"If it isn't my favorite islander," he said as he approached the table.

She turned, her face puzzled before breaking into a smile. "Will!"

He smiled back. "Sorry – I didn't mean to interrupt. I just wanted to say hi."

"You're fine, you're not interrupting. This is Jade, my sister. Well, step-sister, but I like her."

Jade smiled. "Hi!"

"Nice to meet you."

"And this is Morgan, my – "

"I'm sort of like a sister, too, just not blood related." She stuck out her hand, which Will accepted. "Would you like to have a drink with us?"

His eyes darted to Amanda, whose expression remained unchanged. "Oh – no, that's all right. I don't want to spoil sister night."

"Oh please, I insist." Morgan patted the seat next to her – the one across from Amanda.

He looked around. It would be nice to spend time away from his laptop. "Well...that's really nice of you. Saves me an hour wait for a table."

Jade nodded. "Oh yeah, this is a really popular spot. Do you like beer? The beer here is great!"

"Sure, I like everything!" He accepted the menu that Jade handed him and glanced through the drink list. He hardly ever drank alcohol unless he was meeting with a client – rarely just when socializing with friends.

Not that he and his friends socialized often either...they usually combined hangouts with work events. Or they tried to get him to agree to another clubbing disaster.

Amanda cleared her throat. "So Jade – Will is the guy that I spilled that coffee all over."

"Oh no!" She bit her lip. "I heard about that. It sounded bad."

"No, it wasn't that big of a deal; water under the bridge. Amanda has been a huge help in connecting me to contractors and reliable vendors on the island."

"She *is* a wealth of knowledge," Morgan said with a smile.

"Yeah, I don't know about that," replied Amanda, setting her drink down. "Did you finally get to talk to some people?"

"Yeah, just this week. Things definitely move slowly on the island."

"Oh man, I could talk about that all day," Jade said with a laugh. "We've been trying to open a new state park. Er, did Amanda already tell you about it?"

He shook his head. "No, I haven't heard anything about that. But it sounds challenging."

"It has been," Jade said, face bright. "But at the same time, we're so close. And it's been so rewarding. I won't bore you with it, though."

He leaned forward. "Please – I'd love to hear more."

It was a long story, but one that Will appreciated. Jade was much more soft-spoken than Amanda, but seemed more outgoing. Or at least, she offered information more readily. It sounded like she had her hands full with this park, and with her position as head of the committee.

"Were you appointed by the county council?" he asked, sitting back. "Because I've already made some enemies there."

Jade laughed. "I wouldn't worry about that too much. They're prickly with newcomers. Let me know if I can help."

"Oh – thank you. I really appreciate that."

Jade smiled. "I'm going to go to the restroom – be right back."

When she was gone from the table, Morgan leaned forward. "So this is awkward, but we all live together and *technically*, Jade doesn't know that Amanda is thinking of selling the house, so please don't say anything."

Will's eyes darted between them. "Oh – well I'm glad that I didn't bring it up."

Amanda leaned in. "I mean – it's not – it's just something that – "

"It's okay Amanda, you don't have to explain yourself to me," he said gently.

She smiled, looking over her shoulder. "I'm still figuring things out."

"Maybe I could stop by and see the place sometime? Brainstorm some ideas together?"

"You know what," said Morgan, "Jade and I actually have plans tomorrow afternoon, so she'll be out of the house. Tomorrow might be good?"

Amanda let out a sigh. "I mean, I don't know if Will has time for that."

"I have time. Just tell me when."

She sighed, hesitating again before answering. "All right. Then...five?"

"Perfect."

He didn't have long to chat with her after that, because Amanda finished her drink and announced that they needed to get going. She seemed to be in a good mood – better than she'd been on the ferry, at least. Maybe she was finally warming up to him?

The next day, he arrived at her house at five o'clock, as agreed. Amanda met him at the door.

"Welcome to my humble abode," she said as she opened the door.

He took a step back to take the property in. "This is gorgeous. Do you have neighbors?"

"Not really, we've got three acres of woods around us. Nothing crazy, but it's nice."

"This is great, and so private. Thanks again for having me over."

"Of course. Come on in."

The house wasn't huge, but it was modern enough and well-maintained. Amanda led him around, first through the living room and kitchen, then down the hallway to the bedrooms.

In the hallway he paused, catching sight of a wall of picture frames. Some were older pictures – obviously of Amanda when she was younger, along with someone he assumed was her brother. Some were more recent and had Jade, Morgan, and a bunch of other people he didn't recognize.

"I'm guessing this big, scary looking guy is your dad?" he asked.

"Yep." She laughed. "That's him, the source of all my charm."

Will smiled. He thought she was incredibly charming. He was about to walk away when another picture caught his eye. It looked like...a mug shot? "Who's that?"

Amanda grabbed the frame off of the wall. "Oh – no one. It's just a joke that my dad likes to play. He prints out mug shots from work. He, uh, thinks it's funny to replace pictures with them. To see if we notice."

"If I didn't know any better, I'd think that looked just like one of my clients."

"Oh really? That's funny."

She walked past him and showed him the rest of the house. The tour went far too quickly for his taste, and he found himself standing in the living room again.

"I must say, this is a beautiful house. There's a lot of potential here – that is, *if* you want to sell or rent. I totally understand if you'd prefer to keep it to yourself."

Amanda shrugged. "Maybe it'd be good to rent it out? You know, for a little extra income. I could check out some of your other properties, see how it compares."

"Sure." He paused. It didn't sound like she was sold on the idea and he didn't want this to be the last time he got to see her. He took a deep breath. "I must admit that I have intentions completely outside of the real estate realm."

"Oh?" She said, taking a step back.

"I was hoping that you might want to go to dinner with me."

"As your...client?"

He looked down, then back up at her. Was she trying to give him an out? A hint that she was going to shoot him down? "Ah, no. Not necessarily. You don't need to be my client. We can just be...friends."

"Listen Will," she said, "I just – I think that – "

He put his hands up. "No pressure. None at all. I was looking forward to seeing the house, but more so, I was looking forward to seeing...you. I don't know anyone else out here, so it can get kind of lonely."

She frowned. "I know the feeling. I had a rough time when I first moved to London."

"Yeah," he said, shaking his head, "I mean, obviously I know that I'm an interloper here and the islanders want to run me off with pitch forks, but – "

"No, it's not like that. Not really." She laughed. "Okay... sure. Why not."

He smiled. "Great. Are you free...tonight?"

"Oh, like right now?"

He shrugged. "My social calendar is totally open. So...yes. Today! If you're free. Or tomorrow. Any day."

"Not one for playing hard to get, are you Will?"

He laughed – both at himself and at her calling him out. "Not really."

She looked at her phone. "Well, all right. Other than answering angry emails from my boss, I didn't have any plans tonight. Where should we go?"

"You're the expert – what do you think?"

She smiled. "I've got some ideas."

Chapter 10

They had dinner at Amanda's favorite seafood restaurant in town. She agreed to let Will drive – there was no sense in taking two cars – and she was unsurprised to see that he drove a sleek black BMW.

It wasn't until they were enjoying an appetizer of local oysters that Will admitted that he was "new" to seafood.

"What do you mean by new?" asked Amanda.

"Well," he said, reaching for an oyster. "This might be the first oyster that I've ever had. So I hope I'm not allergic."

Amanda's jaw dropped. "Are you serious? Should I be concerned? Do you have a history of allergies?"

He tapped his chin with the oyster shell. "Not really. Just tree nuts, shrimp, wheat, eggs, shellfish..."

Her eyes widened and she snatched the oyster from his hand. "You can't eat that, then!"

He laughed. "I'm just kidding. About the allergies – I don't have any. But I'm not kidding that I've never had an oyster before, so who knows how I'll react."

"I see," she placed the oyster back on his plate and crossed her arms. "You were just testing me, then."

"Testing your reflexes, yes." He scratched at the oyster with his fork before dislodging it from its shell.

His form wasn't great, but he had the general idea. She watched as he placed it into his mouth. "And?"

"Your reflexes were impressively fast," he replied, mouth full. "I was pleased with the results of my test."

She laughed. "No, I mean the oyster. What do you think?"

"Oh. I think they forgot to cook mine."

The look on his face made her laugh again; she even surprised herself with a little snort. "Sorry, I thought you knew these were raw oysters."

"Ah." He set his fork down and straightened out his napkin. "I didn't realize. I think I wasn't expecting the texture."

She nodded, taking another oyster for herself. "It might be an acquired taste."

"Rubbery sea snot? Yes, it must be."

She laughed again, covering her mouth so that the oyster wouldn't shoot out. "Well, I did grow up here, so I don't know what it's like to try all of this stuff as an adult."

"Yeah. My parents wandered into a Red Lobster once during my childhood – it was for my aunt's anniversary party. They left hungry, as did my sister and I. We're more of a chicken tender sort of family."

"If I'd known that, I would've taken you somewhere else. Or at least gotten them prepared differently – you can get them pan fried, broiled..."

"Oh, *now* you tell me?"

She laughed. "I am sorry, Will."

"Don't be," he said with a smile. "Everyone raves about them, I wanted to give it a shot. Not for me."

Amanda decided to splurge on her meal and got the seared scallops, and Will ordered something safe – the fish and chips.

They were both happy with their meals and in the end, Amanda made sure to get separate checks, taking the appetizer onto her bill. She didn't want Will getting any ideas that this was a date.

They were there as friends, that was all. Truth be told, she was grateful for his company. Despite having a lovely evening with Rupert on Thursday, Amanda hadn't heard much from him since. She had hoped that he might suggest a weekend activity, but he never did. They were still chatting over text, which was nice, so she told herself not to rush things.

After Will dropped her off back home, she retreated to her email and set her mind to seeing Rupert again. She managed to contrive a reason for needing to work at the Seattle office that week.

It was easy enough to do – Erica answered her email within the hour and agreed that having her on site for the client meetings on Tuesday and Wednesday would be helpful. Amanda also asked one of her work friends to let her crash on her couch Tuesday night, so she wouldn't have to come all the way back to San Juan both days.

She then mentioned to Rupert that she would be in the office on Tuesday and Wednesday, and he suggested that they do lunch together.

Perfect!

Amanda felt like she was back in London again, restarting her life, and falling in love.

Except this time, she got to play the role of tour guide, telling Rupert about the history of Seattle. She was used to him knowing everything about everything, but now she was in charge.

That Wednesday, she took him to lunch in Pioneer Square; she got to tell him all about the Great Seattle Fire of 1889 – how over twenty-five blocks of buildings burned down, and when they were rebuilding, the city decided to raise the level of the streets by over twelve feet to get above the high tide mark.

This left the remaining store fronts and buildings *under* the new street level; there were stairs to get down there now, and a company even did tours on "The Seattle Underground." Amanda showed Rupert some pictures and offered to take him on one of the tours so he could weave through the underground passageways himself.

Rupert found the history fascinating, and agreed that they should pick a date to go on the tour together. Amanda's heart soared and she took a chance, asking him what he might like to see on San Juan Island.

He hesitated before responding. "You know that I want to see where you grew up, but it's such a long trip, and I've got so much going on here right now."

"Of course, I mean it's no rush, it's not going anywhere. I just think it'd be fun," she said. "Maybe on a weekend when you've got some free time?"

"Sure, that would be nice."

It was hard for her to not suggest that they hang out that following weekend, but she managed to keep quiet. She waited to see if he suggested any sort of plans, but by Saturday afternoon, it became clear that he had other things on his mind.

He'd signed up to do a bar crawl with some of his coworkers, and though he invited her along, it wasn't enough time for her to get into the city – especially with traffic.

"I wish you would've told me sooner," she texted him.

"I'm sorry – it was a spur-of-the-moment sort of thing. Maybe next time?"

"Yeah, definitely!"

She had kept her evening clear in case he wanted to hang out, even turning down a trip on her dad's boat with Jade, Morgan, Matthew, and Margie.

Now she felt silly – why had she waited around for Rupert like that? She should've just taken the initiative and invited him! Surely he would've enjoyed a boating trip? Though he may not have wanted to spend time with her dad...

No, he wouldn't have liked that at all. They'd met in London, but it didn't go exceptionally well. It would be stressful for Rupert, and she knew how much he hated being smothered by her. He once told her, exasperated, that she could be "too much."

It hurt to hear, but she knew he was right. It was a big reason that he pulled away from time to time; he'd tell her that she was being cloying and that he needed more space.

Amanda was *not* going to fall into that pattern again. She'd give him all the space he needed this time.

Another message popped up on her phone – her heart leapt until she saw who it was from.

Will.

"I saw that there's a back-to-back screening of *Tommy Boy* and *Black Sheep* at the theater in town – any interest in going with me? I'll buy the popcorn."

She smiled. She loved Chris Farley movies. Well, her parents had always loved his movies, and she and her brother Jacob got to watch them, too. Chris Farley was a pillar of her childhood.

While she knew that she really shouldn't be spending every weekend with Will, what else did she have to do? Was she really going to text her dad and admit that she wanted to be picked up in the boat? What if Morgan said something about her waiting around for Rupert?

Amanda didn't want to deal with that. She picked up her phone and typed out a response. "That sounds...kind of amazing. What time?"

He picked her up for the six o'clock screening, and afterward they went to a different seafood restaurant. This time, Amanda chose a place that was a bit more touristy – somewhere with more fried options for Will.

He was thrilled, telling her that he was happy to confirm that he no longer suspected he might have a shellfish allergy, and that he was even starting to like some of the stuff.

Amanda made mental notes about the menu – she knew what Rupert liked to eat, so maybe when he came to visit, she could take him there too. He was a big fan of fish and chips, though she didn't know if he would like the "American version," or if he'd complain too much.

The next week, Amanda decided against manufacturing a reason to work in the Seattle office, and instead waited for Rupert to suggest something on his own. It was hard, but she didn't want to push him away by annoying him.

Her waiting paid off. He said that he might have time to come to the island on Sunday, and Amanda was elated. She sent him a list of potential activities – hiking, restaurants, bike riding – and told him to pick whatever he liked. He promised to get back to her by Saturday.

Unfortunately, on Saturday evening, Amanda started feeling under the weather. At first, she cycled between feeling hot and cold; she reasoned that she was just tired, and went to bed early.

When she woke up on Sunday, though, there was no denying it – she was sick. Sick as a dog, and she could barely get out of bed. She sent a text to Rupert letting him know and he responded an hour later.

"I'm glad you texted me early," he wrote. "I was getting ready to leave soon. I'm going to cancel the trip – I can't afford to get sick right now. But feel better!"

It was a letdown, but there was nothing she could do about it. Amanda spent the morning shivering in bed and running to the bathroom. Around one o'clock, she was awoken from her slumber by another text message.

Maybe Rupert decided to come after all?

No, it was just Will. "There's a new ice cream place that just opened – Mountain Berry Scoops. Have you heard of it? They do that rolled ice cream. And regular ice cream, too. Want to swing by today?"

She groaned. The thought of ice cream made her stomach churn. "I wish. I've got some kind of a stomach bug and haven't gotten out of bed all day. I feel awful. Rain check?"

"Oh man, sorry to hear that. I hope you get better soon!"

She fell back asleep and was awoken some delirious number of hours later by a knock at the front door. Luckily, Morgan was home and she answered it.

Amanda laid in bed, trying to listen, but was barely able to open her eyes; her body felt like it had been squished under a rock.

Morgan talked to the person at the door for a minute, then came back to Amanda's room and knocked softly at the door. "Amanda? Are you alive?"

"Yes," she grunted.

Morgan poked her head through the doorway. "Will just stopped by to drop some things off for you. I told him you're too sick to talk."

"Thanks." She had to clear her throat a few times – it was extremely dry.

"It looks like there's some chicken soup, ginger ale, and...a tub of ice cream?"

Amanda had to sit up in bed to get a better look. "Wait, what?"

She shrugged. "Yeah, he gave me a big bag of stuff. I'll put it away for you – or do you want something now?"

"No, but thank you." She cleared her throat again, realizing that maybe she did need to drink something. "Actually, I'll try some of that ginger ale."

Morgan handed her two of the cans along with a card. "Rest up," she whispered as she closed the door. "Let me know if you need anything."

"Thanks."

Amanda took a deep breath. It seemed impossible for her weak body to open a can of soda right now, but she managed to do it. The first few sips didn't go down easy, but after that she could drink a bit.

When she was sure that she wasn't going to need to rush to the bathroom, Amanda opened the card. The front was a picture of two oysters. She opened it to see the inscription. "Heard you were feeling clammy. Get well soon!"

She cracked a smile. Beneath that was a handwritten note from Will. "Hey Amanda, I'm sorry to hear that you're feeling under the weather. I would like to lie and say that I made you my mom's chicken soup, but I'm a terrible cook. I bought the soup in town. I also got you some ice cream from Mountain Berry Scoops for when you're feeling better. Hopes for your speedy recovery. Yours, Will."

Amanda stared at the sloped letters of his handwriting as a hot flash echoed through her body.

Was her fever breaking? Or...had things just suddenly gotten complicated?

Chapter 11

He sent a message to Amanda once he got back to his car. "I hope I didn't wake you up with my visit – Morgan was nice enough to take some snacks for you. I hope you feel better soon!"

Will then drove back home and was disappointed to see there was no response by the time he got there. Maybe she was still asleep?

Yeah, that was probably it. There's nothing like a GI bug to wipe a person out completely.

He got to work on some listings for the first three properties that were ready to be rented. Two were long-term rentals, and one was a vacation home that would only be available a few months a year.

These were the properties that needed the least amount of work – just a coat of paint, or maybe a small fix here or there. Will had hired a photographer to take some high quality pictures, and now he was ready to release them to the world.

Some of the other properties needed more extensive changes; it could take weeks or months before they were ready. Unfortunately, he had no idea about the status of his biggest client's properties. Lenny still didn't want him to stop by or check on anything, even though Will stressed that he'd be happy to line up contractors for whatever work was needed.

Lenny kept repeating that the tenants didn't like to be disturbed, and that he would let him know when he was ready for his help.

They hadn't completed the sales on all of the properties, and Will didn't want to step on Lenny's toes – these were multi-million dollar deals. He could be patient.

Around nine o'clock that evening, Amanda finally returned his text. "Thanks for dropping that stuff off – it's really nice of you. I'm only just waking up now."

"Yikes, sounds like you got it pretty bad. Are you feeling any better?"

"Yeah, I think a bit. I may try to eat something."

"That's good news!"

He scolded himself – he shouldn't text her so much, he was probably waking her up. He left her alone for the rest of the night, but he did text her again on Monday to see how she was feeling. She said she was doing much better, well enough to get her work done from home.

By Wednesday, Amanda reported that she was back to normal, and Will was tempted to ask her out to dinner that night. He'd been having so much fun with her – from dinners, to walks along the water, to that movie night just before she got sick. He was trying to build the courage to ask her to be his date to the company masquerade ball.

Normally, DGG held a yearly party for its employees, and a separate one for clients and friends. It was a way for them to show off to potential investors that they had "style, smarts, and capital," as his boss put it.

This was the first year they were doing an additional masquerade ball. They had a new VP in marketing and she came up with what she called "golden ticket ideas."

Would it cross a line to invite Amanda to be his date? Or would she assume that he was only after her as an investment?

He really wanted to make it clear that he didn't care – not really – about her house. He was interested in her as a friend... or, more than a friend.

Amanda was skittish, though. Every time he inched toward the "more than a friend" designation, either by asking her out two nights in a row, or trying to pay for her meal, Amanda abruptly pulled away.

It was subtle, but he caught onto it. She'd start to stutter or mumble, or try to change the topic. But when they just hung out as friends, went to dinner, joked and laughed, she was fine. He hated to ruin it by crossing that line.

But at the same time, he was starting to wonder if it was *time* to cross the line. There was a certain point where he could no longer deny how he felt, and he'd have to decide if he was willing to risk losing her friendship for the chance of having something more.

Was he at that point with Amanda, though?

He didn't have to think on it for long. The sick feeling he got when he thought of her, alone and ill, completely helpless, told him all that he needed to know.

True, she wasn't *completely* alone or helpless – apparently Morgan was there. Maybe Jade, too.

But still. He was worried about her, and even briefly considered learning how to make soup for her.

That was it. He made up his mind to call her on Thursday when he knew she'd be feeling better. He wouldn't let himself back out of it. One way or another, he'd invite her to that masquerade ball. The rest was up to her.

Chapter 12

It really seemed like there was a Starbucks on every corner in Seattle. Mike didn't mind – he quite liked Starbucks. No one questioned him sitting there with a single order of coffee for hours at a time, and the coffee was delicious.

There was a Starbucks across the street from the Dirk Gold Group building. It gave Mike excellent visibility of the main entrance, and of an exit-only stairwell.

There were other ways to get in and out, of course. But the guy he was interested in – Lenny Davies – wasn't careful about his comings and goings. Ever since Mike arrived in Seattle two weeks ago, he spent many of his days camped outside of the office, waiting for Lenny to show up.

Lenny had only been in twice, but that was enough. Mike was able to follow him – disguised, of course – and place a tracker on his car.

Lenny had never been one of Sabini's brightest, which made him easy to follow. But it also made Mike wonder what Sabini was entrusting him with. Amanda seemed to think that he was going to sell properties to them, but why?

Maybe it was something minor – something not worth the time of one of Sabini's main guys? The timing was odd though, and the location. Only a few months after his arrest on San Juan Island, and Lenny was back for more?

There was just something about it that didn't sit right with him and he couldn't let it go. That, and the fact that this was the only lead he'd gotten since leaving the FBI.

Though Mike still had friends in the FBI that he could reach out to if needed, he wanted to wait until he had something solid. There was no use kicking up dust and attracting attention to himself before he knew what was going on.

So far, he hadn't found out much.

When he looked through recent sales on San Juan Island, he didn't see anything under Lenny. There were some companies that owned buildings, but it was impossible to trace them back to Lenny or to the Sabini family. They could literally belong to anyone.

Mike also found the apartment where Lenny was staying – a fancy high-rise downtown. There was some security and cameras set up in the building, but nothing substantial. After watching it for a day, Mike was confident that he could get into the building. There were a lot of tenants with dogs, so he was thinking that he might need to rent a dog for an afternoon. Was that a thing? It had to be. It would help with his cover and with getting in.

He was still getting used to Lenny's pattern of movement. Since he didn't have anyone to be a lookout for him, he had to be extra careful when he broke into Lenny's apartment to plant the bugs. It was vital that no one was there when he entered or when he was leaving.

According to the information on DGG, there was going to be a party thrown in two weeks' time for the company's investors and "friends." Lenny, the shrewd mastermind that he was, responded on Facebook that he would be attending the party.

Mike couldn't one hundred percent count on that, but it was the best plan he had for now. He wanted to get something on Lenny's computer too, if he had enough time. So far, Mike hadn't been able to crack Lenny's communications at all. He'd considered using the coffee shop's WiFi to hack into Lenny's phone, but Lenny never seemed to be craving a coffee when Mike was snooping around.

That was a let down, but Mike was okay with waiting. Lenny was sloppy. Whatever was going on, Mike would figure it out in the end.

For now, he had to wait for that party.

Chapter 13

"Are you *kidding* me?" Morgan said as she threw her arms down at her sides.

Amanda closed her eyes. "No, I'm not. But it isn't that simple, I don't – "

"Of course it's that simple! First of all, you might get more information about Lenny. And second of all, it's a *masquerade* ball! Do you know what I would do to get into a real-life masquerade ball?"

"Oh yes, we all know," Jade said with a smile.

Amanda sighed. After Will had invited her to be his plus one at this company ball, she broke down and told Jade everything. She felt guilty that Will had dropped off all of that stuff when she was sick; she felt guilty that she'd hidden things from Jade; and most of all, she felt guilty that Will seemed to...care about her.

"I honestly don't get the problem," Morgan said.

"I'm starting to feel...weird about all of this," Amanda said slowly. "I feel bad. I don't want to lead Will on."

"He's a rich jerk who only cares about money. You said it yourself! And obviously, if he's willing to work with someone as scummy as Lenny, then he's questionable too."

"That's not true," said Jade. "He may not know anything about Lenny. He might just be trying to do his job. And I don't know, Amanda. I think that...well, that he really likes you."

"Who cares!" Morgan said, standing up from her seat on the couch. "What part of scummy goon are you not seeing! Also, do you think that there's any way I can get an invite?"

Amanda laughed. "I don't think so."

Jade continued. "And I'm not so sure that Will is a jerk. What about all that stuff he brought over when Amanda was sick?"

Morgan waved a hand. "That's just salesmanship. Like when your realtor buys you a bottle of champagne after you close on a house."

"How many houses have you closed on?" asked Amanda.

"Uh, none," Morgan said, crossing her arms. "But I have friends. And I've seen things! He's just...a really good salesman."

"Maybe." Amanda sat for a moment, staring at Jade, who was suddenly entirely too quiet. "What is it, Jade? You think that this is all a terrible idea, don't you?"

"I wouldn't say *that*." Jade shrugged. "I just think..."

"What? You can say it."

"Well, it seems like you've been having a lot of fun with Will. You guys are always hanging out, and he seems willing to drop everything to spend time with you."

Amanda shook her head. "Like Morgan said, it's probably just him being a charming salesman. And besides, I'm not interested in Will. Rupert and I have been patching things up."

Jade and Morgan shot a look at each other.

"What?" Amanda said, hands on her hips.

"I hate to admit it, but Jade's right," Morgan said. "You've spent a lot more time with Will than with Rupert. We've never even seen the guy."

"He was *going* to come up and visit, but then I got sick. And he's very busy."

"We just don't know Rupert," Jade said gently.

"Well you don't know Will either," Amanda said. "Morgan, you make good points. This party could be a treasure trove of information. I have to go."

Morgan squealed. "Yes! Now are you *sure* that you don't want to ask Will if I can come?"

Amanda laughed. "I'm sorry, this is a one-woman mission." She looked at Jade, who was still sitting with a perturbed expression on her face. "Don't worry Jade – nothing bad will happen. If I see Lenny, I'll just get out of there."

"It's not that," Jade said with a faint smile. "I just...I don't know. Good luck."

"Thank you."

Amanda pulled out her phone and gave Will a call; he picked up quickly and she told him that she was happy to accept his invitation to the masquerade ball.

The ball wasn't for two weeks, though, and Amanda made up her mind to avoid hanging out with Will until then, and instead try to prioritize Rupert.

She worked a few days in the Seattle office, again crashing on her friend's couch, and went to lunch with Rupert four times. One evening, they went to dinner, too. Things were going well. Rupert was still exceptionally busy, but he was making time for her. That was important.

No, he hadn't made things official yet. Amanda didn't want to ask about it. It was his effort that mattered, and it meant something. She wouldn't push it for now.

She did mention to him that she was going to a fancy party, and that she technically had a date – a friend, but a date nevertheless. He laughed, seemingly undisturbed by this. "Since when do you like going anywhere fancy?"

She ignored that comment; she knew that he was probably being rude because he couldn't say what he was thinking.

Secretly, she'd hoped that he might decide it was time to name her his girlfriend again, but that was silly. He spent a lot of evenings and weekends hanging out with his friends – many of them ladies. He'd made a lot of friends in his short time in Seattle; Amanda couldn't help but notice. And she couldn't help but pine after him.

Oh, so much pining. It wasn't healthy, the pining, but she felt powerless to stop it.

When it finally came time to go to the masquerade ball, Amanda was nervous. She wasn't so sure that it was a good idea anymore.

Morgan loaned her a mask, which was nice of her, but kind of odd. Why did Morgan have a mask despite never having gone to a masquerade ball? Another Morgan mystery.

It was a pretty, delicate thing – white with lace and tiny jewels, and asymmetrical so that the right side of her face had a dramatic sort of flair. When she put it on, it made her feel mysterious. Maybe there was something to this masquerade stuff?

It was also a useful disguise in case she saw Lenny. Hopefully, she would look nothing like herself. Maybe she could even creep around and eavesdrop without him knowing?

That might be a stretch.

She took off the mask and slipped it into her purse before getting into her car. The plan was to meet at Will's place in Seattle, and then leave together from there. Amanda was surprised when he sent her his address; he didn't live downtown, but in Licton Springs.

He seemed like the kind of guy who would want to be where all the action was. She thought about that the whole way there. Maybe he'd bought a house here?

That might be it. He might be flipping a house or two; prices were skyrocketing everywhere.

Yet when her GPS told her that she'd arrived, she didn't think she'd come to the right spot. The house was big but looked like it was falling apart; the front steps were partially caved in.

Amanda picked up her phone and sent him a text message. "I think I'm here? But maybe I went to the wrong place."

A moment later, the front door opened and he waved at her.

Odd. This wasn't what she expected at all. Amanda unbuckled her seat belt and got out of the car, suddenly self-conscious about how fancy this dress was.

"Welcome to my humble abode!" he said. "You're a bit early. Would you like to step inside for a tour? Or a drink, or something?"

She *was* curious as to what it looked like on the inside. "Sure."

She stepped inside and Will introduced her to the woman sitting on a rocking chair in a nearby room. "Mrs. Holland, this is my friend Amanda."

"Hi there," Amanda said with a wave.

"You're going to have to speak up," the woman replied. "You're facing my bad ear."

Raising her voice entirely too loud, Amanda repeated, "Hi there!"

The lady nodded, blinking her eyes slowly before returning to her knitting.

Will shot Amanda a smile. "This way to the kitchen."

Once they were out of earshot – although, considering Mrs. Holland's poor hearing, they were probably always out of earshot – Amanda asked, "So...is that your grandma or something?"

He laughed. "No, she's my landlady. She's owned this house for, oh I don't know, a hundred years? I rent a room upstairs from her."

"Oh."

"I've been trying to slowly fix things up for her. She has a son, but he lives in Oregon and can't help much. Oh I'm sorry – can I take your coat?"

"Sure," Amanda said, unbuttoning the black peacoat and handing it to him.

"I'm just going to come out and say it," he said in a way that made Amanda's heart skip. "You look stunning."

She smiled. There was that salesman. He almost had her for a second. "You don't look so bad yourself. Is that the suit that I almost ruined?"

"Similar! But no, this is my 'fancy' tuxedo. Nothing's been spilled on it. At least not yet."

"Is that a dare?" she said with a laugh, taking a seat at the kitchen table.

"No, I already know you can do it. What would you like to drink? A glass of wine, water, beer...a margarita?"

She looked around. "I wouldn't expect Mrs. Holland to have a full bar."

"Oh yes. She has a drink every night at seven. Just one. Her doctors keep telling her that she has to stop, but she refuses. She says that she hasn't gotten to this age by following their advice."

Amanda laughed. "I'm surprised that she shares this information with you. And in that case...I guess I'll have a margarita?"

"Coming right up! And she doesn't exactly tell me these things," he shook his head, a half smile on his face. "I drive her to her appointments and they assume I'm her grandson. It wasn't technically part of our deal, but the first month I was here, she nearly took out a neighborhood kid while driving. Ever since then, I drive her wherever she has to go."

Oh my gosh. Was he serious? Was this his real life?

Since when was Will...selfless? Driving this woman around, fixing up her house?

Why had she ever listened to Morgan!

"Are you okay?" He set down the lime squeezer.

She shook herself out of it. "Yeah, sorry. Just spaced out for a second."

He eyed her for a moment before returning to his drink-making duties. "Okay."

"Can I ask why you decided to stay here? I don't mean to be rude, but the way that you talk about money, I thought you'd live somewhere – "

"Nice?" he suggested.

Amanda smiled. "No, just – you know, fancier."

He nodded. "Yeah. Well, that's the thing. This place is good enough. I'm on San Juan a lot now, and like I told you, my dad's back injury ruined his business. So I've been paying for my parents' mortgage for the past couple of years. And I help my sister out too – she's in school. She has some bad spending habits that they can't support." He laughed to himself, "Honestly, I shouldn't be supporting those either, but she's almost through."

AMELIA ADDLER

Oh dear. Oh dear oh *dear* oh dear. So not only did he take care of this strange, unfriendly lady – he took care of his entire family too?

Maybe he only liked Amanda because she, too, was a strange, unfriendly lady!

No. He was nice to her because he was a nice person. Morgan had been wrong. This whole plan was wrong. She shouldn't have come here, tricking him into taking her to this ball so she could spy on Lenny.

She swallowed, feeling her throat drying up. Amanda was the lowest of the low. Scum of the earth. Will was a nice guy – what was she thinking?

She felt the room spinning and reached her shaky hand to take a sip of water.

Will had been distracted and missed all of this. After a moment, she managed to choke out a response. "What's she going to school for?"

"Dental hygiene," he said over his shoulder, shaking the drink shaker. "She had a tough time when she was younger; she went to the community college after high school, but she ended up dropping out. Had a rough few years after that, but now she's doing what she wanted to do."

"Wow."

He slid the margarita in front of her. "What?"

"Ah. I don't know. It's just that...you're like a saint or something."

He laughed. "Hardly."

She had to find a way to get out of this party. Maybe she could fake another GI bug? No, that would be questionable since it happened so recently. "Listen, I don't know that I can go tonight. This isn't really my scene."

"Oh come on, it'll be fun. And if it's not, we can leave. And do whatever you want to do. I'm sure there are tons of places that we could get a decent dinner."

Ah. She wasn't going to get out of it that easily. "Well I'm not – the thing is..."

"Let me see your mask. Wait – I'll show you mine."

He disappeared for a moment before coming back into the room in an all-black, Phantom of the Opera style mask. "Pretty cool, right?"

"Yeah. Really cool." She took a sip of the margarita.

"Where's yours? If you don't have one, they'll have some at the ball – "

She shook her head. "No, I have one. It's Morgan's, actually. I just feel silly."

"Let me see."

She sighed and pulled the mask from her purse, slowly tying the ribbon behind her head.

A smile broke across his face. "You are absolutely beautiful."

Now Amanda really felt like she was going to be sick. "Will, I really don't think – "

"Listen, I get it. It's a stuffy event. I told my boss I was coming, so I just need to pop in for twenty minutes, say hello. And then we can leave."

"I just..." Her voice trailed off.

"Please? For me? Your favorite stalker?"

Her throat was totally dry. She took another sip of her drink.

She hated herself so much in this moment, for so many reasons. "Okay."

He clapped his hands together. "Okay? Okay! You won't regret it."

Chapter 14

He yelled goodbye to Mrs. Holland on his way out, then took Amanda out back where his car was parked under the crumbling carport. Hopefully she wouldn't judge him too harshly for that.

"Please excuse this dilapidated structure," he said, opening the passenger door for her. "I was going to fix this, but then I realized that she shouldn't be driving anyway. So now, I just park my car under here and pray that it doesn't collapse."

"Yeah, that wouldn't be good."

"Especially because this is a company car. Pretty sure my boss would murder me."

He got into the driver's seat and started the car. "Traffic can get tricky around this time of day. I was thinking that we could take the bus in? There's a station not too far from here. Unless you're opposed to wearing your ball gown on the bus."

"Ha, it's not a ball gown." She shook her head. "And no, I don't mind at all. That sounds smart."

They got to the station quickly and had to rush to catch the next bus, which arrived at almost the same time they did.

They made it on and despite the bus being nearly full, they managed to get two seats together. Will felt a bit absurd being so dressed up, but as per usual with public transportation, no one seemed to notice or even look at them.

He shot a look at Amanda. She was being unusually quiet – maybe she'd preferred driving but didn't want to say anything to him?

No, that wasn't like her. Amanda wasn't afraid to speak her mind.

Maybe she was just dreading this party?

"Look," he said, "I know that big gatherings and parties can be hard for introverts. So you really don't have to go in. I'll say hello to a couple of clients, and we can go to dinner or something."

She shook her head. "No, it's not that. Really."

"Are you sure? Because the look on your face says that you're going to a funeral."

She smiled. "I'm sorry – I'm sure it'll be really nice. I'm excited about it I just...I don't know."

"I was told that there will be all-you-can-eat gourmet food. And twenty-eight thousand dollars worth of flowers."

"Twenty-eight *thousand*!" Her mouth hung open. "How many flowers is that?"

He shrugged. "You'll have to wait and see for yourself."

They got off at their stop and had to walk two blocks to get to the party. Amanda assured him that she had no problem walking the distance in her heels. "I got used to wearing heels when I was in London. I guess it makes me feel fancy."

"Well, you look very fancy."

She smiled, looking down. "Thank you."

Just outside was a red carpet. They paused before stepping onto it to put their masks on. He then offered her his arm.

"Shall we?"

She smiled. "Yes, I'm ready."

They walked in following a group of ten slowly moving people. Will didn't mind; it gave him a chance to admire what had been set up inside. Fresh flowers covered nearly every surface; he wasn't a flower person, but the smell was captivating.

They checked their coats and entered the ballroom. The ballroom itself was beautiful; DGG didn't skimp on the venue. There were tall marble columns topped in gold surrounding the room. He guessed that there were at least two hundred people inside, though it didn't look crowded. Strings of flowers cascaded down from the ceiling, giving the feeling that they were under some sort of enchanted forest.

"You were right," Amanda said, leaning into him. "This is...perfect."

The soft lighting caught a thousand times on Amanda's mask, sparkling and making her shine like a diamond. Will couldn't stop staring at her. If only she wasn't so morose about the whole evening – though now, she seemed stunned into silence as she looked around the room.

Maybe she'd been upset because she was confused about what this party meant? He wanted to tell her how he felt about her – that he didn't care about her house. All he really cared about was her.

But it didn't seem like now was the right time. He wanted her to start having some fun. And there was nothing that improved a mood like good food.

"They're serving dinner in the other room – would you like to get something to eat?"

"Oh yes, that would be great!"

On the way there, they ran into Will's boss, Gordon, and Will introduced them.

"I knew that Will would find *many* precious gemstones on that island," Gordon said, kissing the top of her hand. "But I had no idea just how precious. Nice to meet you Amanda, enjoy your evening."

He walked off and Amanda pulled her hand away, a look of disgust on her face.

Will reached up to rub his forehead, forgetting that he was wearing a mask. "I'm *really* sorry about him. He's...."

"Disgusting." Amanda laughed, covering her mouth with one hand, and holding the other hand in front of her. "I feel like I need to go and wash this off. What just happened?"

Her laughter was contagious. "That's how we all feel when we have to interact with him." Will pointed toward the restroom. "Please, feel free to wash your hands."

"Yeah, I think I will pop in for a second. Be right back."

As Will waited, he cursed himself for bringing her here. He thought it'd be a first-class, grand party and a perfect time to tell her how he felt. Now he wished they'd just gone to get seafood again so she would've been more comfortable and no one would've kissed her hand. That would've been a lot more natural for their relationship.

When she emerged from the restroom, he was prepared to continue his apology. "I'm *really* sorry about him. I wish we could ban him from these things. He's the worst. At the last party, he told the wife of my client that she reminded him of his sister. He specified it was his 'hot' sister."

Amanda groaned. "Oh my gosh, make it stop!"

"Okay, I'm done. Dinner?"

She smiled. "Sure."

They were able to make it through dinner without any further incidents. Amanda seemed to be enjoying herself. Not as much as she enjoyed the Chris Farley movies, but more than earlier in the evening.

Will tried to think of every funny story he knew about the company, and he got her laughing as he pointed out the various characters from his office.

Once dinner was through, he asked her if she'd like to dance.

She hesitated. "I'm not a great dancer."

"That's okay. Neither am I."

"And I don't like people...looking at me."

"Well, my friend, I'm afraid it's too late for that." He stuck out a hand. "No one can keep their eyes off of you."

She looked down, smiling, before accepting his hand. "Fine. *One* dance."

They walked to the dance floor hand-in-hand. There was a big, live band – the company spared no expense in front of their clients.

The music was fast – maybe Glen Miller? His mom always loved that stuff. Will did his best impression of a swing dancer, spinning Amanda out and twirling her back in. She was laughing now, really laughing, despite their missteps.

When the song ended, Amanda fanned herself with her hand. "Okay, I guess this is pretty fun."

"I'm glad you think so."

The next song started, much slower than the first. A woman's voice rang out, singing the opening words to "At Last."

His heart leapt. "I know you only agreed to one song, but would you do me the honor?"

She took his hand and he brought her in close. They swayed gently to the music, his face only inches from hers. It was a nice change of pace from before, but his heart was still thundering in his chest.

This was the moment. This was when he needed to tell her how he felt.

"Amanda, I – "

He was cut short by a voice and a rough grab on his shoulder. "Will! I thought that was you!"

Lenny. Great timing buddy.

Will turned around to shake his hand. "Hey Lenny."

"Good to see you too. How's it going?"

Will nodded. "Good, very good. Let me introduce you to my friend – "

He turned, but Amanda was nowhere to be seen.

He paused. "Hm, not sure where she went."

"Yeah, where is your pretty friend?" Lenny said. "I was hoping for a dance with her myself."

Ha. Will could only imagine what Amanda would say to that. "I'm not sure. She just – disappeared."

Lenny frowned. "How do you know this girl?"

"She's..." Will faltered. He wasn't about to tell Lenny his life story. "One of my new clients."

"I bet I know where she went." With that, Lenny walked off.

That was an odd thing to say. No wonder Amanda disappeared – there were predators all around this ballroom. He stepped off of the dance floor and looked for her.

He was about to take the stairs to the upper balcony when his phone buzzed in his pocket. A text from her.

"Will, I'm so sorry. I have to go. Thank you for the nice evening."

Chapter 15

Mike checked his watch. 20:30. He had been inside Lenny's apartment for over an hour. So far, he was successful in planting a few bugs, but not as successful in cracking the password on Lenny's computer.

There was a surprising amount of security on the laptop. It confirmed what Mike suspected – that Sabini *did* have him doing something important.

If he could only get onto the laptop, he could install a key logger and see everything that Lenny was doing. The password cracker had been running for almost an hour with no luck, though. Mike wished he'd had more time to try to phish the password off of Lenny – he could craft some sophisticated looking traps if he'd had the time.

Too bad. It seemed unlikely that this would work now; he would need hours for the program to run, trying a trillion combinations.

When might Lenny be gone for hours? Maybe Mike could get him arrested again. On bogus charges maybe, but at least he'd be out of his hair for a day or two.

There was movement behind him. Mike turned around to see his decoy dog, Biggles, carrying something in his mouth.

"What do you have there?" he asked softly.

Though the shelter workers told Mike that Biggles was deaf, he seemed to understand things just fine. His stare was unbroken as his tail began slowly wagging.

Mike laughed and reached down into Biggles' mouth. "You're going to have to let it go eventually."

More wagging.

Mike let out a sigh. Whatever it was, he wasn't going to get it right now.

He looked back at the computer – still nothing. His phone buzzed in his pocket; he'd set up a small camera in the building's lobby so that he could keep an eye on anyone coming in. It buzzed his phone every time someone walked past the camera.

So far, there had been no one of importance. But just now, the image on the screen caught his eye.

He couldn't make out the face clearly – it was a guy in a suit. About Lenny's build and height.

Mike clicked back to look at the video thirty seconds before the guy arrived. He caught a glimpse of his face.

Yeah, it was Lenny.

Shoot. He thought that he'd have more time. Now he only had a few minutes, pending the elevators, to get out of here. He quickly unhooked everything and attached Biggles' leash.

"All right boy, it's time to go."

Biggles took no heed of his urgency. He plodded along next to him at his medium-slow speed – it seemed to be the only speed that he had. Perhaps Mike hadn't chosen the right dog?

No. Biggles was the only one for him. Mike had turned up at the shelter planning to put in an application to foster a dog. He just wanted a rent-a-dog to help him fit into the building.

But then he saw Biggles. The poor old guy sat quietly in his cage, paws crossed. He was small, terrier-looking, with wiry grey and orange fur. There was a poise about him; Mike imagined it was confidence.

The staff said that his owner ended up in prison, but brought Biggles in first, begging that they find him a good home.

"Does the owner have a long sentence?" Mike had asked.

"Long enough that Biggles will never see him again," the employee responded. "Poor guy. It's hard to find a home for a senior dog."

That was what hit him. Biggles definitely looked like a senior. His eyes were a bit cloudy, his ears stunk, and his muzzle was entirely white. The staff told him that overall, Biggles was healthy and well cared for – he was just old.

Mike wondered why the owner went to prison. He'd sent many men to prison himself – not directly, but from his investigations. It weighed on him sometimes. It felt like justice was uneven; some of the worst men he'd ever known were walking free, while their minions rotted in jail. The worst criminals, the bright ones, got out of their sentences by making deals and turning in their friends.

What had Biggles' guy done? Was he a peon, betrayed by a less scrupulous friend? Had he hurt anyone?

He had, at least, loved his dog. That counted for something. Mike didn't know how to fix the system. But he could save one dog.

"I'll take him," he'd said.

Now Biggles was his one and only accomplice. They walked out of the apartment after Mike carefully checked that no one was coming. He would've preferred to take the stairs, but Biggles didn't do well with steps and they were on the twenty-fifth floor. He wasn't in the mood to run down that many flights, either.

Mike picked Biggles up, went down two flights of stairs, and then went to wait at the elevators on that floor, hoping they wouldn't run into Lenny.

They stood at the elevator and when the doors popped open, Mike waited a moment before walking over. It didn't seem that anyone was there...until he heard that familiar voice.

"I'm telling you, I saw her! I bet she followed me, I bet she's looking for me! How do you know that she's not following me?"

Mike realized his mistake – this elevator was going *up*. It would be too suspicious to back out now, though. He kept his head down. He had on a hat and fake mustache, which was decent, but they were awfully close for such a light disguise.

They got to Lenny's floor and there was a moment where he stopped talking on the phone, seemingly studying Biggles. Mike stood, eyes focused on the ground.

"Dude," Lenny said as he walked off of the elevator, "your dog *stinks*."

Mike smiled to himself and said nothing. The elevator doors closed and thankfully, they started moving down the building.

Biggles dropped whatever had been in his mouth, apparently tired of keeping up the ruse.

Mike bent down to see what it was. It looked like a key fob for a car, but it was strange. There was no emblem, the entire case was black.

He studied it, noticing a small pinhole near the unlock button.

If he didn't know any better, he'd guess that this was a hidden camera.

"Good job, Biggles," Mike said, patting him on the head.

The doors opened again and Biggles took the first step out.

Chapter 16

Her first thought was to hide in the restroom. Amanda was in there for a few minutes before she realized how silly it was – *eventually* she'd have to come out, and Lenny might see her. She needed to get away from the ball entirely.

Will had responded to her text. "What's wrong? I wish you would tell me what happened. I'm sorry if I upset you, can we talk?"

How could she possibly tell him what was going on? If she told him about Lenny being in the mafia...no, she couldn't. And Will hadn't done anything wrong. It was all her.

He'd been a perfect gentleman – just as he was to his parents (whose mortgage he paid), and his sister (whose education he supported), and to old Mrs. Holland (who he cared for and chauffeured around).

Will had treated her with kindness, and how did she repay him? By taking advantage of him and using him to spy on Lenny.

She tried to form a response to his message, but she couldn't think of what to say. She was having a hard time thinking at all – she needed to get out of this bathroom stall and get back home.

Amanda tried to clear her head. So what if she'd seen Lenny? He wasn't going to attack her out in the open.

Probably.

Plus, she had a mask on. What was the chance that he recognized her?

Amanda was more worried about seeing Will. What would she tell him? What if he asked her to dance again? The way he'd pulled her onto the dance floor, his hand on her waist...

She snapped herself out of it. It was time to leave.

She left the restroom and popped her head around the corner. There was no sign of Lenny, and she spotted Will at the far corner of the ballroom. He seemed to be caught in a conversation with an older looking couple.

Perfect. She quickly walked to the coat check, got her jacket and left the building without anyone noticing her.

The further she got from the ballroom, the less frenzied she felt. By the time she got to the bus stop, she was confident that Lenny hadn't followed her; it would have been too hard for him to blend in without her noticing.

Once seated inside the bus, she decided that it was safe to take her mask off. She also knew that it was time to respond to Will.

She let out a sigh and pulled her phone out of her purse. The first three messages she typed out were silly; she deleted them immediately.

What was she trying to say? She couldn't tell him the truth. He couldn't know about Lenny.

Yet what even *was* the full truth? If it was just a problem with Lenny, she could've told Will that she wanted to leave. She didn't have to leave Will, too.

No. It was something else. It was the way Will looked at her, the way his hands ever so lightly led her on the dance floor. The way he did so much for his family and that old woman...

Plus, even though Rupert didn't care that she was going out with another guy, it felt wrong.

Yeah. That was it. It wasn't the fact that she'd gone out with Will. It was the fact that she was *enjoying* it.

She was almost to her stop. She needed to say something to him.

"You didn't upset me," she wrote. "Things are complicated. I wish I could explain, but I can't. It's honestly not you. I'm so, so sorry."

She got off at her stop and realized that she needed to catch a ride back to Will's place to get to her car. She still had the address saved in her GPS from before; she ordered an Uber and was picked up a few minutes later.

After she got back to her car, the drive to Anacortes went quickly and she was able to get a spot on the ferry back to Friday Harbor.

Her escape was complete. Sort of.

When she was on the ferry, she looked at her phone again. Will had written back an hour ago. And Rupert had texted her – twice!

Will's text said, "I won't push you on it. I got home and saw that your car is gone – did you get home okay?"

This she could answer easily enough. "Thank you, I did. Have a good night Will."

Rupert had texted her almost two hours ago, and when she hadn't answered, he texted again.

The first text said, "Hey beautiful, what're you up to this fine Saturday night?"

Then, "I see how it is, too busy for old Rupe."

She smiled and rolled her eyes. It was unlike him to double text – he was always rather aloof, even when they were dating.

"Nonsense," she wrote back. "I just didn't see your message."

He responded immediately. "And now, you're making me miss you."

A faint smile spread across her face. That was unexpected.

She couldn't think about it, though. Her brain felt fried. Once Amanda got home, she pulled all of the ridiculous pins out of her hair, took a shower, and went to sleep.

———◆———

The next morning, Morgan and Jade were making breakfast when she wandered into the kitchen.

"There she is!" said Morgan. "I thought you were going to stay the night in Seattle at your friend's place?"

Amanda shook her head. "No. I left a little after eight."

"What happened?" asked Jade.

"I don't know. Everything. Nothing." She sighed. "Lenny was there; he walked right up to us."

Morgan's jaw dropped. "Did you tase him again?"

"No." She smiled to herself. Maybe she should have brought the taser – she would've needed a bigger purse. "I didn't do anything. I just ran off. I sent Will a text, got back to my car, and caught the ferry. Just...left."

"Oh, it's okay," Morgan said, taking a seat. "I'd freak out too if I saw Lenny."

"What did you tell Will?" Jade asked.

Amanda groaned. "Nothing. I told him that I was sorry and that I had to go. I can't do this. Now I understand why Connor left the country after dealing with Lenny, like, two times."

Morgan laughed. "Oh come on, it isn't that bad."

Amanda said nothing. She didn't know how to explain it.

"Did you get to see his place?" Morgan continued. "Was it fancy?"

"No, it wasn't fancy." She shook her head. "Not at all. He rents a room from an old lady. He helps her fix things up. Drives her to her doctor appointments."

"Weird." Morgan frowned. "Was he a bad date?"

Amanda buried her face in her hands. "No. He was a *great* date. He told me that I was beautiful and that he couldn't take his eyes off of me. And then I just ran away, like a coward."

Jade placed a hand on Amanda's shoulder. "So...you're saying that maybe he's not as bad as we thought?"

Amanda kept her face buried, her voice muffled. "Yes, it turns out that it's *me* who's been the crappy person all along! Big shocker."

"You're not crappy," Morgan said with a shrug. "You're just on a mission. You're a concerned citizen."

Amanda scoffed and picked up her head. "Yeah right. I'm a jerk who led him on and pretended to be his friend, all so I could run away when I actually saw Lenny."

"It doesn't seem like you were *pretending* to be his friend to me," Jade said with a slight smile.

Amanda rolled her eyes. Sometimes Jade sounded just like her mom. "I've been so focused on Rupert that I didn't really think of Will *that* way. But clearly he thinks of *me* that way! And it's not fair to him, he doesn't deserve it."

"So what are you going to do?" asked Morgan.

"I'm going tell him the truth."

"You can't do that!" Morgan said, her volume rising. "He's going to think you're insane."

"Maybe I am." Amanda shrugged. "And I don't mean about Lenny – about Rupert."

"Oh." Morgan weighed this. "Yeah, that makes sense I guess."

She couldn't take it anymore. Amanda excused herself to her room and sent Will a message. "I'm really sorry about yesterday. I'd like to explain if you had a few minutes to talk today?"

His response came a few moments later. "Sure. I was really worried about you. Is everything okay?"

"Can I give you a call?"

"How about we meet up? Oyster Coffee?"

She let out a sigh. It was cowardly of her to be unwilling to tell him to his face. "Okay. Half an hour?"

"I'll be there."

Amanda got to the coffee shop early, bought a cappuccino and sat at a table outside. Her whole body hurt. She wasn't sure if it was because she'd run so much in her heels, or because she'd slept so poorly – throwing herself back and forth across the bed.

She had a recurring nightmare of the ballroom. No matter how many times she woke up, she'd always slip back into the same dream. In it, she and Will were dancing again, twirling and laughing. But then Rupert would show up, or Lenny would show up, and Amanda would panic and no matter how much she ran, she could never get away.

"Hey."

She looked up. There he was, as promised. "Hi. Do you want to get some coffee?"

"No, I'm okay." He took a seat across from her. "Are *you* okay?"

"I'm fine. I'm just...I should've told you this yesterday."

He put his hands up. "Listen, I'm really sorry that I made you go to that party. I thought it would be fun, I didn't think – "

"It *was* fun. You didn't make me do anything. It was really fun, and you're really fun. But things are complicated for me."

"Oh?"

She shifted in her seat. How could she explain this without explaining it? How would Rupert put it? He was always so good at this sort of thing...

She could at least give him a *form* of the truth. "There's just a lot going on. And I can't tell you about everything."

He let out a little laugh. "Now you're making me nervous."

"I'm sorry. But, see – here's the thing. I'm sort of seeing someone. Someone from my past." That made it sound like he was a ghost, or that it was a civil war romance or something. "I mean, it's my ex-boyfriend. Things have kind of rekindled between us in the past few weeks."

The words registered on his face and he sat back. "Ah, I see."

"And there are...other things, but I can't talk about them."

He sighed. "If it was something I said, I'm sorry, I – "

"No." She set her coffee down. This wasn't going great. But if Will knew that Lenny was with the mob, he probably would dump him as a client. Except Amanda couldn't tell him that. "It's about Dirk Gold Group. I don't think they're the kind of company you want to work for."

"Because my boss is a creep? I mean, I know that he can be a bit weird, but he...just has a bad personality."

She shook her head. "No, it's not that. It's – something else. But it doesn't matter. I think that you're too good for that company."

He laughed. "Well, a job is a job."

"And I think that you're too good for me, too." There. She'd said it. Amanda stood up. "I'm sorry Will, I really am. I don't think we should spend time together anymore."

He raised his eyebrows. "I'm sorry too. I had no idea – I really enjoyed our friendship. I wouldn't want to lose that."

She couldn't stand to look at him, or the shock in his eyes. "I'm sorry, Will. I don't know if I can...I don't know. I have to go. Take care."

Amanda picked up her coffee, throwing the remainder in the trash. She couldn't stomach it. She couldn't stomach any of it.

At least it was over now.

Chapter 17

Sunday morning was hectic for Margie. First, she met with two clients who wanted to tour the barn; then she dropped off a donation for the library bake sale, and finally, she had to pick up a few more ingredients for the Sunday dinner that evening.

When the girls arrived, Margie was rushing around. The stuffed peppers still needed fifteen minutes in the oven, and the potatoes were nowhere near soft enough to be mashed; she cursed herself for not cutting them into smaller cubes.

Perhaps she'd tried to fit too much into one day?

"Hi Mom!" Jade said brightly, giving her a kiss on the cheek. "I made a blueberry cobbler for dessert – is there room for it in the fridge?"

"Of course – whatever space you can find is yours."

"Anything for me to carry in?" asked Morgan.

Margie sighed. "Unfortunately, no. I'm a bit behind schedule today."

"Oh sorry, can I help?" Morgan asked, stepping up to the sink to wash her hands.

Though it *would* be a help if they set the table, Margie preferred that they sit down and relax. "No, it's okay. Everything's fine. Hank should be home soon, and hopefully he'll bring Matthew with him."

Morgan frowned, peeked out into the dining room, and announced, "You know what, I'll just set the table."

There was no point in protesting – Morgan had seen right through her.

"Thank you dear."

Margie realized that she had let the sauce sit for too long and it burned a bit. Darn it! She gingerly stirred it and turned down the heat. She'd wanted to make extra sauce for Hank – he liked the peppers to be swimming in it, and then he'd dunk bread in there, too. Hopefully she hadn't ruined it.

Once the stuffed peppers were done, Margie turned off the oven and covered them with foil so they wouldn't dry out. It was another ten minutes before the potatoes were ready to be mashed, and that was when Hank walked in the door, armed with flowers and an apology for being late. At least her timing meshed with something!

When she finally got everything onto the table, Margie sat and stared at the food. It looked fine, but she'd completely lost her appetite.

"What have I missed?" she asked, passing around the stuffed peppers.

"I was just saying that I don't know that Luke will *ever* come back," Morgan said glumly. "He's having too much fun in Vancouver."

"You say that like it's a bad thing," Hank said, a smile on his face.

"It *is* a bad thing!" Morgan said with a laugh. "He does that to you. He annoys you so much that when he's gone, you feel his absence."

"Don't worry," said Jade. "He'll be back in a few weeks."

"Where's Matthew?" Margie asked.

"He just texted me," Jade replied. "He's on his way. He got a little held up on a call."

"Oh okay."

Morgan let out a dramatic sigh. "I guess I'll just keep playing third wheel to Jade and Matthew forever."

"You're not a third wheel." Jade made a face. "I thought we had fun together?"

"We *do*," Morgan said. "But you know what it's like. Or maybe you don't. Three's a crowd."

Only three? Margie frowned. Why wasn't Amanda spending time with them, too? She hoped they weren't leaving her out. She made a mental note to ask Jade about it later.

She realized that Amanda hadn't said anything since she'd arrived. "What about you, Amanda? How is everything going at work?"

"Everything's...fine. Good, I guess."

Oh dear. It did not *sound* fine. Maybe the girls weren't getting along?

Margie shot Hank a look, but he was focused on buttering a slice of bread.

She cleared her throat. "It sounds like you've been working in Seattle a lot more frequently. That must be stressful."

Amanda shrugged. "It's okay."

"It's only because she wants to spend more time with Rupert," Morgan cooed.

Now Hank's interest was piqued. "Rupert? What does he have to do with Seattle?"

Morgan's face fell. "Oops. I'm sorry, I thought everyone knew."

"It's fine," Amanda said. "It's not a secret. Rupert's working in Seattle now. He took a transfer. We get lunch together sometimes."

Hank jabbed his fork into a stuffed pepper, nearly collapsing its sides. "Lunch, eh?"

"Come on Dad, we're allowed to be friends."

"The last time that the two of you were friends, you ended up – "

"It's *fine*," Amanda said, setting down her fork. "It really is. It's not like we – "

Morgan gasped. "Jade. What is that *thing* on your finger?"

Jade's hands darted under the table. "Oh, Matthew was supposed to have gotten here by now..."

Margie leaned forward. "Yes Jade, what's on your finger?"

Jade let out a sigh before pulling her hands up from under the table and resting them both in front of her. On her left hand was an unmistakably glittery and shiny new ring.

Now Margie gasped. "Jade! Who gave you that?"

She laughed. "Well, we wanted to tell you all tonight – he just proposed yesterday – I think he should be here any second – "

Margie jumped up from her seat, as did Morgan and Amanda.

"Proposed! Honey! Did you say yes?"

"Of course I did!" Jade laughed. "I said yes right away. I suspected he was up to something, he was acting so strangely."

"Who *wouldn't* say yes to that ring," Morgan said, pulling Jade's hand closer to her face. "Who helped him pick this out? He definitely didn't come to me. Amanda?"

She shook her head. "Not me either."

Margie turned toward Hank, who was sitting back with his arms crossed over his chest.

"Hank? Did you know about this?"

He didn't answer at first, looking innocent.

"*Hank.*"

"You ladies think we can't do anything right," he said, smiling broadly. "But between me and Matthew, I think that we picked a pretty decent ring."

"And you didn't tell me!" Margie said. "How could you keep it a secret?"

"Because," he set down his napkin, "I didn't think it was fair for you to find out before Jade did."

"But *you* got to know!"

"Only because Matthew was worried he'd picked the wrong ring."

Just then, the front door opened and Matthew walked in. He was immediately confronted by Margie and Morgan who asked a hundred questions about the ring, the proposal, and when the wedding would be.

"We haven't had time to plan any of that yet, but we'll figure it out. I don't want anything big."

"I don't mean to be pushy," Margie said, "but I happen to know a very nice barn right here on San Juan Island."

Jade smiled. "I was hoping you would say that. But I don't want to take time away from your real customers."

"Nonsense!" Margie threw her hands up in the air. "You can have the barn every weekend for all I care!"

After the excitement died down and everyone left, the exchange between Amanda and Hank floated back into Margie's thoughts. As they were getting ready for bed, Margie brought it up again.

"Why did you attack Amanda about Rupert? It's hard to get her to talk to begin with."

Hank sighed. "I can't help it. He's a jerk. I can't believe she's even speaking to him again."

"Well...they're just getting lunch."

"No way. He's up to something. She was like a zombie after he broke up with her the first time. It seemed like she was finally getting back to normal, and then he shows up again. Typical."

Margie frowned. It was true that Amanda had been morose about the breakup – but it also seemed like her mood had improved in the recent weeks. "She didn't seem very happy at dinner tonight. I was worried that Jade and Morgan were leaving her out or something."

"No." Hank shook his head. "I doubt that's it. Rupert always makes her unhappy. He always did, and now he's come all the way to Washington to continue his mission of making her miserable."

"Well...she's a smart girl. She'll figure it out."

"I don't know what to say to her," Hank continued. "It seems like she ignores all of my advice. She shuts down."

Margie laughed. "Of course she does, you're her father. She's not going to be eager to take your advice on love and relationships."

"I have some experience, you know. In relationships. I'd like to think that I'm a pretty good husband."

Margie stopped what she was doing to look at him. He was in a tizzy; his face was even getting red. She went over and gave him a hug, patting him gently on his back. "Of course you are. You're a wonderful husband."

"I thought that if I was a good male role model, that she'd be fine. That it would all work out."

Margie laughed. "If only it were that easy. Maybe she's still in love with him. It's hard to see anything clearly when you're in love."

"I wish she could see that she deserves better," he said, shaking his head.

"Me too. Maybe she will. Maybe we can help her."

"Good luck with that." He shut off the light next to his bed and rolled over. "I've been trying for years."

Margie smiled to herself. Her techniques were a bit more subtle than Hank's. Plus, she had allies in Jade and Morgan – they might be able to help Amanda most of all.

"Don't worry sweetie – I'm on it."

Chapter 18

The rest of the week did not get any better for Amanda. Since she'd spent so many days in the Seattle office trying to see Rupert, she ended up falling behind on a project at work. Their midpoint presentation was due soon, and Amanda had to work sixteen hour days all through the weekend to pull things together.

She told Rupert about all of this, and he sympathized. They were having issues with the new server and he was working a lot of late nights, too. It made Amanda feel a bit better – at least they both had a reason why they couldn't hang out on the weekend.

Amanda went into the office the following Wednesday to deliver the presentation. It went well, and she suggested to Rupert that they celebrate by getting dinner together.

"Sorry babe, can't do it. Things are still too hectic. But maybe next week?"

She smiled. He called her babe! He hadn't said that in ages.

"Okay, just let me know."

She was doing her best to play it cool, but she was starting to wonder why he hadn't brought anything up about them being "official." True, he hadn't done more than hold her hand on a few occasions and give her a kiss goodnight, but it felt like *something* was going on between them.

She was doing everything that she could to keep him from feeling stressed, and hopefully it would pay off. But at the same time, her stress level was through the roof.

Will had texted her twice that week, just to say hello and check in. She was polite when she responded, but she kept things light. She had done enough damage leading him on, and she didn't want to be responsible for any more harm.

That next Saturday, she was again waiting by the phone, hoping that Rupert would tell her he was coming up to visit sometime that weekend, when Jade popped into her room.

"Hey! How's it going?"

"Not bad, how about you?"

Jade shrugged. "Can't complain. Morgan's doing a wedding today, and Matthew's working. I was thinking about going for a hike – do you want to join?"

"Oh. Hm. Where are you going?"

"I'm open to suggestions. It's such a nice day that I was thinking of going over to Orcas Island. I'm sure we could see for miles from the top of Turtleback Mountain."

Amanda instinctively picked up her phone – no new messages. It was already eleven, wouldn't Rupert have told her if he were coming up today? "I do love the view...but I hate the climb."

"We don't have to do a mountain. What about a hike around the lake? Cascade Lake is one of my favorites."

"Ah..." Amanda looked around. She hadn't put much thought into leaving her room yet, and this seemed a bit much. "I'd probably just slow you down."

"You're not going to slow me down! Come on. Do you have hiking pants? Jeans? Put on some pants."

"Oh my," Amanda laughed. "I'm not used to you being so stern."

Jade pulled open a drawer, and after finding it filled with socks and pajamas, shut it again. "I don't know where they are, but I'm sure you have some."

"Yes, I have pants."

Jade crossed her arms. "I'm not going to let you sit here and sulk all day."

"I'm not sulking," Amanda replied, a bit too defensively, as she stood up.

"Okay, I'm sorry. Not sulking. But you have definitely been down ever since the masquerade ball."

Amanda shrugged. "Work has been busy."

"Come on. Put on your jeans and we'll talk it out."

Amanda groaned. "Aw man. I'll only put them on if you promise to not make me talk it out."

Jade laughed. "Okay, whatever you want. Let's go, we need to be in line for the ferry in twenty-five minutes."

She looked at her watch – it was now or never. There was no point in sitting around in her room all day by herself; she'd recently been feeling like she was missing out on all the fun. She told herself it was because of work, but that was only a partial truth.

Amanda went over to her closet and pulled out a change of clothes. "I'll be ready in five minutes."

"Great!"

They made it to the ferry and enjoyed a peaceful ride to Orcas Island. The sky was clear today – clear and blue. Amanda peered out of the wide ferry window and admired the way colors became more vivid through her sunglasses. She wouldn't admit it to Jade, but the blue skies were cheering her up, even if only a little bit. It was enough to get her to put pants on, which was a win.

Once docked, they drove to Moran State Park and started on the trail. They were twenty minutes into their hike when Amanda started to feel like she was actually enjoying herself.

She suspected it was partially because she'd put her cell phone into her backpack so that she wouldn't check it every fifteen minutes for a message from Rupert.

It was helping her relax, and true to her promise, Jade didn't ask anything about Rupert at all.

So naturally, Amanda started babbling.

"I just don't get what his problem is."

"Who? Lenny?"

Amanda shook her head. "No, Rupert. He's been living in Seattle for weeks. At first it seemed like things were going really well, but now..."

"Not as well?"

"No. I mean, things are progressing, I think. We're texting a lot, and we see each other at the office sometimes. We'll go to lunch, and we've done a couple of dinners. I guess I don't know what I expected. Maybe I just expect too much; we weren't even really speaking for months before."

"I see."

An eagle flew overhead; they both stopped to look at it as it settled in a faraway tree.

Amanda began again. "When he first moved here, I tried not to get my hopes up. But when we went to dinner, he basically said that he'd come here to reconnect with me."

"What else did he say? Like did he say that he'd missed you, or that things have been hard without you around?"

Amanda let out a sigh. "No, but he doesn't say stuff like that. It's not his style."

"You could just ask him."

She shook her head. "I could, but I know he doesn't like it when I smother him. I'm just trying to be considerate."

Jade nodded. "But do you think he knows what you want? That you want to be together again?"

"Yeah, he has to. I mean, it's been a few months since I said anything about wanting to get back together, but it's pretty obvious. I just don't want to force the issue, you know?"

Jade stopped and pulled a water bottle out of her backpack. "From what I'm hearing, it sounds like you have to sort of tiptoe around him?"

Amanda shrugged. "I wouldn't call it tiptoeing, it's – "

"But it sounds like you do a lot of things to prevent him from being...scared off."

"It's not 'scared off' exactly, it's just so that he doesn't feel trapped or anything."

"Trapped into what, though? Into being in a relationship?"

Amanda thought for a moment. That wasn't quite it. "I don't know."

"Do you worry that if you ask him about it, he'll be scared of being in a relationship with you again?"

"Not exactly." Amanda let out a sigh and looked down at the lake. The water looked gorgeous and inviting, despite the chilly temperatures. When she was growing up, she spent summers cliff diving into the blue waters of the lake with her friends. That's something that Rupert would love – if he'd just give it a chance. And if he was still around in the summer.

Jade was staring at her. She spoke again, her voice soft. "I think the question is – why are you so worried that he'll be scared off?"

"Because I'm scary!" Amanda said with a laugh. "You know that. Everyone knows that."

"You're not scary! You're witty. And straightforward. But you're *not* scary."

Amanda looked down at her feet navigating the roots and rocks on the trail. How could Jade ever understand? She was as sweet as they come. She probably never scared a guy off in her entire life.

That just wasn't how things were for Amanda. She had a lot of bad qualities. She joked about taking after her dad, but it wasn't always funny. She could be overly harsh; she had trouble sharing her feelings.

Back when her dad started dating again, Amanda was so unnecessarily nasty to Margie – one of the nicest women on earth! All because she couldn't face her own feelings about her mom's passing.

Amanda still felt guilty about that. She felt guilty about a lot of things. Rupert knew these parts of her, and he was okay with them. Who else would put up with it?

Jade was a good person – she didn't know what it was to have dark parts of her soul that needed to be hidden.

"Will wasn't scared of you," Jade continued. "And I think that's despite your best effort to scare him off."

She laughed. "Will doesn't count."

"Why not?"

"Because he was trying to buy my house."

"Was that all?"

Amanda didn't want to think about it – another thing she felt guilty about. "Who knows."

Jade was quiet for a moment. "You know, I don't want you to get mad at me for saying this."

Amanda stopped walking. "What?"

"But you remember that I was divorced, right?"

"Yeah, of course. I remember."

Jade glanced at the ring on her finger for a moment before looking back up at Amanda. "My ex-husband Brandon was... not that nice. I'm not bitter, and I don't still hold things against him. But he just never – I don't know, he never put me first. He never treated me well."

"Yeah, he was an idiot. He messed up."

Jade nodded. "I'm not saying that Rupert is as bad as my ex-husband but...the thing is, I knew that Brandon wasn't that good to me. Deep down, I mean. I never said it out loud. But there was some part of me, and I can't explain why, that thought it was the kind of treatment that I deserved."

"Aw, Jade!"

She continued. "I don't think that anymore. Things with Matthew are wonderful – like unreal. Better than I thought was possible."

Amanda smiled. They were a great couple. "That's lovely."

"But I had the same feeling with Brandon. I had to walk on eggshells all the time, it was always my fault if he was in a bad mood or things weren't quite right. I was always catering to him, and never questioning why he didn't do much for me." Jade cleared her throat. "The thing is, it's true what they say – we often accept the love that we think we deserve."

"So you're saying that I let Rupert blow me off because I think I deserve that?"

"No. Please don't get mad. What I mean is – think of it this way. What if Matthew was doing those same things to me – not making the commitment, keeping me waiting. What kind of advice would you give me?"

Amanda shrugged. "That's different, you and Matthew don't have a history like me and Rupert."

"That's true," Jade replied.

They hiked in silence for a few minutes before Amanda changed the subject. Jade simply didn't understand Rupert.

Why should he stop everything he was doing to pay attention to her? All while he had this new part of his career that he was trying to get off the ground?

Plus, Amanda wasn't exactly a peach. There weren't a lot of guys out there who were going to put up with her. Rupert understood her, he loved her. At least, he used to love her.

He held her hand when she cried about her mom, he listened to her sob. He was the only one that she could talk to, the only one she could open up to.

He understood her, ugly bits and all. That wasn't something she was willing to risk just because she was impatient about their status as a couple.

No, Amanda wasn't going to try to explain that to Jade. It was embarrassing.

When they got back to the car, Amanda was excited to find that she had a new message on her phone.

Her heart fell when she saw that it was from Will. "How're you doing on this beautiful day? I've been running around like crazy all week, but I got the okay to check out some of my new properties. Would you have any interested in seeing them with me and finding people to fix them up? I could really use the help."

The guilt hit her again. That was the original agreement, wasn't it? That she would help him navigate the small town politics of the island.

She'd left him hanging there, too.

She and Jade had a pleasant trip back and decided to get a pizza. As they ate, Amanda asked her opinion on seeing Will again.

Jade considered it as she took a bite of pizza. "Hm. You *do* kind of owe him."

"That's what I was thinking. I can make it clear that we're just friends."

"I think you've been quite clear with him."

"Hey!" Amanda laughed and tossed a paper straw across the table. "What's that supposed to mean? Are you saying that because I haven't been clear with Rupert?"

Jade laughed. "No, I'm not talking in code. I just mean that you flat out told Will that you were seeing your ex. Right?"

"Right."

Jade shrugged. "So...I think you're good there."

Amanda smiled. It would be nice to see Will again – and it would make her feel less guilty if she could help him in some way.

She answered his message. "I'm happy to help! When are you thinking?"

Chapter 19

The latest property added to the DGG portfolio on San Juan Island was an impressively sprawling, though neglected, estate. There were two enormous houses settled on twenty-two acres of beachfront property. The previous owner got into trouble for tax evasion, and somehow DGG was able to snag the entire thing for a cool $2.2 million.

Will estimated that it was worth closer to $7 million, all told. The houses were both impressive, over six thousand square feet each. They were planning to convert both of the homes into lavish vacation rentals, while also squeezing in a few more homes and cabins on the property for the lower budget guests.

Will had the idea to add a building in the center to act as a sort of community center for all of the properties, with an indoor pool, gym, and movie theater; he was determined to make it an entrancing place to stay regardless of budget.

He'd walked through the property briefly before, but today was his first chance to take his time and brainstorm. There were some obvious problems – the landscaping was overgrown, there were fallen trees obstructing walkways and one of the driveways, and worst of all, the homes had both been left unin-habited for years.

It was nothing that he couldn't manage – their inspections revealed no *major* issues. And truth be told, Will knew who to hire for all of this work.

No, that wasn't exactly true – he wasn't happy with the landscaping crew he'd hired for another project. They showed up four days late, overcharged him on mulch, and then had the audacity to bill him for overtime weekend hours.

So his appeal to Amanda wasn't a lie. It just wasn't entirely innocent, either. Ever since the night of the ball, he'd been telling himself that he needed to give her some space. She made it clear that she was in a relationship – or *something* – with her ex.

But why had she called him her ex? Why didn't she just say that she had a boyfriend? Maybe since they'd broken up once, they'd break up again...

Was it Amanda taking things slow? Or the ex-boyfriend? Because if it was him who was dragging his feet in getting back together with Amanda, then he was an idiot.

That might not be the story, though. The questions ran around and around Will's head until he was able to rationalize seeing Amanda again.

He needed a new landscaper. She probably knew all the reliable ones. It was as easy as that.

Plus, this estate was stunning – she'd want to see it. He'd texted her some pictures and she was intrigued.

She'd written, "I knew that these kinds of places existed on the island, but I've never actually been inside one of them. This is really interesting."

"I have some pictures of it back in its heyday too – they're a good comparison as we plan the renovations." He sent those pictures along as well, and Amanda said she was looking forward to the before-and-after pictures.

Will smiled to himself. There – she was hinting that she'd like to hear from him again, months from now, when the renovation was done. Even if Amanda had a boyfriend, she was still his only friend on the island. He valued her for her friendship alone, and he'd leave it at that. He wouldn't bring up his unwanted feelings again.

They agreed to meet on Sunday at noon. As he stood on the property, feeling overly hot in the sun despite the cool breeze, he wondered if maybe she would back out of coming. This was a much lower-key hang out than the ball, though; she wouldn't have to worry about prying eyes or his unsavory boss. It was just the two of them.

A few minutes after twelve, he spotted her car creeping up the long driveway. He waved, trying to keep his smile from being overly enthusiastic, as she parked and opened her door.

"Hey! You made it!"

Amanda stumbled over some debris as she stepped out of her car. "I did. This is...something. I didn't realize that this driveway would go back so far."

"Yeah, sorry about that. The GPS just takes you to the tip of the property. When they say it's an estate, they mean it's an *estate*," Will said with a laugh.

"They really do," Amanda replied, looking around.

"As you can see, it's gotten a bit overgrown here. What used to be a well-maintained garden turned into a sort of jungle."

She nodded. "When I was coming in, the grass was almost as tall as me. I wanted to get out and check, actually. Was that intentional? Is it supposed to get that tall? Why would they plant that kind of grass?"

Will shrugged. "I have no idea. That's actually what I wanted to ask you about – if you knew anyone who could help tame it. My landscaper turned out to be a dud."

"Hm. I might. It seems like half of the guys from my high school tried their hand in the landscaping business. I can ask around from some friends and neighbors and see which company is worth hiring?"

"That would be *great*, I really appreciate it."

She smiled, then slowly turned in a circle, taking in the surroundings.

Will stood there, watching her. She was all buttoned up now – her black coat zipped to her chin, a puffy scarf around her neck. There was no long gown, no mysterious, sparkling mask. But she looked just as beautiful as she had the last time that he'd seen her; just more closed off. He let out a sigh.

"Is everything okay?" she asked, turning toward him.

Whoops. Didn't mean to do that so loudly. "Yeah, just you know – there's a lot to do here. Shall we?"

"Sure."

He unlocked the door to the first house and they walked into the expansive foyer. The marble floors looked dull and dusty, and the grand staircase had a faded carpet tumbling down, torn in spots.

"It's a bit of a forgotten place."

"Yes, but I can still see that it was so *glamorous*," Amanda said. "The high ceilings, the lighting, and the detail on the banister...it's incredible."

Will smiled. "I agree. It's a little rough around the edges, but it's all about how you look at it."

"How you look at it," she repeated, nodding. "And how much are you selling this for? Can we do a house swap?"

He laughed. "If it were up to me, I'd give it to you. But unfortunately, the plan is to use this place to make as much money as possible for DGG."

"I thought you ran that place," Amanda said with a smile.

"Ha! Yeah right. I'm still a nobody. But if all goes well on these projects, I have a good chance of making partner."

Amanda turned to him, eyes wide. "At DGG?"

"Yep, the one and only. I've been working there a while. I'm pretty young to make partner, but I put a lot of time into the company and brought in impressive clients. I'm handling all the clients here on my own."

"I see."

"I didn't think that I would end up spending my whole career at one company, but things move fast at DGG. Faster than any other investment groups where my friends work. So I guess I'm lucky."

Amanda nodded and turned away, walking into the next room.

Will cringed at himself. He didn't mean to sound like he was bragging – not at all. He was trying to acknowledge that he knew it was odd that someone his age could make partner – but DGG was a different kind of company. They were growing so fast that there was room for him to move up. Or maybe Amanda just had such a low opinion of the company that she thought it was a bad idea?

He wasn't sure. They walked into the kitchen, the exquisite tile work standing stark against the blank holes where all of the appliances were supposed to be.

Will cleared his throat. "The guy who owned this property is in prison for tax evasion – but before he went, he stripped the place of whatever he could. He didn't even leave a single toilet in this house. I mean, how much could he have gotten for old toilets?"

"The appliances he could resell," Amanda said as she uncrossed her arms, running her fingers across the marble counter top. "But the toilets – he took those to send a message."

Will laughed. Of course she was right; he hadn't thought of it that way. "Good point. And send a message he did. There are *eight* bathrooms in this house. And wait until you see the other house – it's even more extravagant."

"That's wild. What kind of job did this guy have?"

"Beats me," Will said, walking into the next room. He was excited to show this one to her – it was an enormous library with bookshelves from floor to ceiling. There were two levels connected by a copper spiral staircase, and a rolling ladder that spanned the room. "He took the toilets but left all of these books behind, so I wouldn't say that he was an intellectual."

"Clearly he had other priorities." Amanda laughed. "This library is the most impressive room yet."

Will smiled, watching her climb up on the ladder. He didn't want to disappoint her in telling her that his boss wanted to strip the library bare and turn it into a game room. Will was going to argue that the bookshelves needed to stay.

"Hey look, I'm Belle from *Beauty and the Beast!*" She threw out an arm in an attempt to make the ladder roll. It moved an inch, then jolted to a halt. Amanda nearly fell off, but she grabbed onto a rung and caught herself.

Will burst out laughing. "Are you okay?"

"I'm fine," she said, her cheeks flushing pink. "Just trying to dislocate my shoulder. You might want to put some oil on that."

"Noted." He smiled. "You know what's cool – there's a secret passageway in here."

"Get out!" she said, jumping off of the ladder.

"It's a little rickety – behind this book shelf. It leads to the kitchen."

She nodded. "A shortcut to snacks while you read. What could be more perfect?"

They peered into the passageway, but Will advised against walking through it.

"I'm not sure how safe it is, we have to get the engineer in there to make sure it's sound."

"Ah, I see. Maybe the engineer can disguise it better, too."

He frowned. "Yeah. I think it blended in better before the shelf bent the hinges. Maybe the books were too heavy."

Amanda shrieked. "I think I just saw a mouse!"

"Yeah, you probably did." Will shut the door. "There are some critters that took up residence on the property. There's a cat, too. I caught a glimpse of her outside, but she ran off. I'm guessing she's been living off of mice and birds. She basically owns this place."

"What's going to happen to her now that you're invading her kingdom?"

Will smiled. "Nothing. She can keep living here. She'll be the new landlady. I'll put it in the brochure."

They then toured the second and third floors. In one of the master bedrooms, Amanda opened the balcony door and stepped outside, revealing a gorgeous view of the water.

"So he went to jail for tax evasion?"

"Yes," Will said, joining her on the balcony.

Amanda leaned forward, hanging her hands over the balustrade. "A normal person would be satisfied with all of this. They wouldn't need *more*."

Will smiled and leaned his back against the railing. "For some people, nothing is enough."

Amanda spun to face him. "Are a lot of your clients like that? Where nothing is ever enough?"

"No, I wouldn't say that." He shrugged. "Some are normal. Some are even nice people. But sure, we have our fair share of people with insatiable greed. It's kind of unavoidable in the finance world. No one goes into finance to help people."

Amanda frowned.

Oh no – what had he said? He hurriedly added, "Not everyone, though. One of my clients is a big philanthropist, and he ended up donating a bunch of land for wildlife conservation. And he – "

"What about...the really bad clients?"

"What do you mean?"

Amanda looked down, then out to the ocean. She was clearly struggling with how to word her thoughts.

"It's okay, you can say it. You're not going to offend me."

She flashed a smile. "You promise?"

"What do you mean, the really bad clients?"

"I...might know one of your clients. I saw him at the ball."

"Oh really?" That would explain why she got so upset. "Who was it? How do you know them?"

She bit her lip. "It's complicated. I can't tell you."

"Well, who is it? Maybe I can tell you how bad of a person they are. You know, like on a scale of one to ten – one being someone who volunteers to pet bunnies at the animal shelter, and ten being...I don't know, the guy who designed those automated sinks that only work when you walk away."

"I can't tell you who it is. But I can tell you that he's in the mafia."

Will felt like she'd just hit him. He was *not* expecting that. "What? How do you know people in the mafia?"

"I don't *know* him – it's complicated. But there were some issues here on the island. You remember that my dad's a cop, right?"

"Yes..." he said slowly.

"I mean, it can't be that hard to figure out who it is if you vet your clients. I know they use shell companies and launder money, but if you look under the hood, you'll see that something isn't quite right."

He eyed her. Was this some kind of joke? He didn't do business with the *mob!* "Oh, is that all? Just look under the hood?"

"I'm not saying that you're going to go on their property and it's going to have a bunch of drugs out in the open or something. But also, I don't know that that's *not* the case? We're pretty close to the Canadian border, and that might be useful for drug smuggling..."

"Whoa whoa whoa, what're you talking about? Who is this client?"

She shook her head. "I can't tell you."

"What kind of mob are you talking about? Like guys who sell fur coats that fell off the back of a truck? Or like...guys who will kill me if I mess something up?"

"I don't know, I'm not privy to any of their business. But I'm sure that they do illegal stuff, and make a lot of money doing it. And I know that you sympathize with – "

"I don't sympathize with the mafia!" Will took a deep breath. He realized that he'd sort of shouted. "I'm sorry, I didn't mean to raise my voice. But it feels like you're accusing me of being something that I'm not."

"I'm not accusing you of anything. I just don't think you know what you're dealing with."

He walked back into the house, determined to walk away and regain his composure.

"Or *who* you're dealing with," she added.

He spun around. "Is this really what you think of me? That my clients are mafioso's and I'm this bad dude who helps them launder drug money? Or are you just making this up to keep pushing me away?"

"No, I don't *know* that it's drug money, it could be from other stuff. You know – whatever they do."

He dropped his arms to his sides. "So you have no idea what this client does, but you're *sure* that he's in the mob, and you won't tell me who he is. Oh, and I'm possibly laundering drug money. Really helpful Amanda."

She stormed past him and stopped in the hallway. "This is why I couldn't tell you. You don't care about the truth. Like you told me the day that we met, all you care about is money."

His jaw dropped. "That is not what I said!"

"Good luck with this house!" she said as she ran down the stairs. "I'm sure you're going to make a ton of money off of it!"

The front door slammed shut and Will stood there, looking down the crumbling staircase, her words echoing in his mind.

Chapter 20

It took a moment for Amanda to realize where she was and how to weave through the overgrown brush to get back to her car. This stupid estate was way too big.

Once she got to her car, she slammed the door with a huff and started the engine.

At least now she knew that Will was happy to do business with the mob – and probably other criminals.

She bounced down the long driveway, annoyed by the fountain and the lion statues near the exit. This place could've been used in a movie – it looked like a criminal's lair. How could Will not see that? How could he not question these things?

When Amanda got home, she was surprised to see that she had a message on her phone.

Her heart leapt. Was it Will, apologizing? She fumbled putting her password in.

But no, it was Rupert. "How about we play hooky tomorrow and I come up to visit the island?"

She smiled. "Play hooky? I don't know, I have a lot going on at work."

"Come on. We all do. When was the last time that you called off sick? It'll be fun."

Amanda had *never* called off sick. There was even a time when she spent the night in the emergency room, so ill with a stomach bug that she'd gotten severely dehydrated. They gave her an IV of fluids and some medication so she would stop throwing up, and the doctor told her that she should rest or she'd end up admitted to the hospital.

But the entire time, Erica was angrily texting her, telling her that she shouldn't let her team down and that they had an important meeting the next day. Amanda attended virtually, looking as put together on camera as she could, while stealthily turning her camera off when she had to be sick.

If she hadn't called off *that* day, then she wasn't going to pretend to be sick for no reason at all!

But on the other hand...this was the first time that Rupert actually *wanted* to come to San Juan Island. If she said no, then he'd accuse her of not being spontaneous – a criticism that was often true. She could always catch up on work later...

"Okay," she finally wrote back. "It's on."

She spent the rest of the day cleaning up around the house and planning for Rupert's visit. It was a good distraction for her – she only thought about Will a mere two dozen times or so.

That was better than expected. Amanda was a world-class brooder. She could dwell on something for weeks before saying a word about it. There were things she brooded on for years, even!

The more that she replayed their conversation in her head, though, the worse that she felt. Obviously she couldn't tell Will that the mob client was Lenny, and that she'd been forced to assault him once. But how could he think that she was just making it up as an excuse to push him away? That was ridiculous.

If she wanted to push him away, she'd just...do that! She was an expert at pushing people away! She didn't need excuses.

Maybe he would think about it and realize that she was right. Or maybe he wouldn't, because his livelihood depended on him keeping his eyes and mouth shut.

She'd promised him those landscaper recommendations, though, so despite feeling awkward about it, she solicited a few names and texted them to him at the end of the night. She ended the message with, "I'm sorry about our argument. I didn't mean to offend you."

He wrote back, "Don't mention it. And thanks for the recommendations."

Drats. Clearly he hadn't gotten over it yet, or changed his mind.

Oh well. At least she'd told him the truth. If he didn't want to hear it, that wasn't her problem. She wasn't going to waste any more time thinking about it. At least now she could stop feeling guilty and move on with her life.

Rupert arrived the next morning on the early ferry. Amanda was giddy with excitement – she'd texted him a list of restaurants ahead of time, and he picked one for lunch and a different one for dinner. What if he loved the island? If things went well, she could surely bring up their status as a couple – maybe ask him what he envisioned for the future?

Initially, she thought that she might be able to make dinner for him, but he'd never liked her cooking, and she didn't want to spoil the day.

They got lunch at a place on the west side of the island that was known for their excellent seafood.

Rupert, however, wasn't terribly impressed. "You'd think that the food would be fresher being so close to the ocean."

"I mean, you did pick the lobster. We're not known for our lobster."

"You're not? Oh – is that another part of the States?

Amanda giggled. "Yeah, Maine. About as far from Washington State as you can get. We're famous for our Dungeness crab, not lobster."

He laughed, popping a shrimp into his mouth. "My mistake!"

After lunch, they went for a walk along Fourth of July beach. It seemed like they were having a pleasant enough time, and Amanda was just so excited that he was there.

"This was my mom's favorite beach," she told him.

"I can see why, it's nice."

"It's been really strange knowing that she'll never come back to these places. And I feel like...I don't know, guilty? Because in some ways, it's like I'm starting to forget her."

"I don't think you could ever forget her."

She nodded. People always said things like that, but it didn't encompass what she felt. She'd never tried verbalizing the thought before, though – and she was struggling. "Not forget that she existed. But it's like...I used to think about her every day, and miss her every day. I still miss her, don't get me wrong. But now it's like she...I don't know, she doesn't take up as much of the space in my mind."

"So you're finally able to move on with your life?"

"I guess. But it feels wrong. Like a betrayal, or that I care less."

He let out a sigh. "I don't know what you want Amanda. Do you want to get over her death, or do you want to be a mess for the rest of your life?"

She took a step back. She wasn't prepared for him to say something so...harsh. "I don't *want* to be a mess, I'm just saying that, you know, the more okay that I feel without her, the worse I feel about it."

He shrugged and kept walking down the beach. "If that's how you choose to think about it."

Amanda stood there, trying to piece her thoughts together. Maybe Rupert was right. Instead of questioning or having doubts about finally getting over her mom's death, she should just move on with her life. She shouldn't overcomplicate things, she shouldn't spend so much time looking back.

She frowned, turning to look out over the water. That didn't seem quite right, though. For a moment she thought she might cry, but she was able to stop herself.

No need for Rupert to think she'd lost her mind. The wind whipped around her, and for a moment she imagined that it was making her stronger. Despite the gusts of air, she was firmly planted on this beach. She wasn't going to tip over or fall to pieces. It ripped through her hair, and though she knew her hair would be a ball of knots later, Amanda didn't care. The icy touch on her cheeks made her feel like she was on the edge of the world.

She looked up from the rocks at her feet to see that Rupert was a good distance away. She shook her head, sure now that she wouldn't cry, and jogged to catch up to him.

For dinner, Rupert had chosen Amanda's favorite restaurant on the island.

"So," she said, hands on her hips. "Was that the best meal you've ever had, or what?"

He shrugged. "It was good. I'd say it was 'island good.' Not as good as a restaurant in Seattle."

"Really?"

He reached across to hold her hand. "Sorry dear. It can't compete with a major city when it comes to quality. There's no competition here – there's nothing to strive for. You probably love it because you've got sentimental memories associated with it, and that's fine. But it's not objectively great."

She let out a sigh. "Ah. I see."

"Don't take it personally," he added. "It's kind of how you are with this whole island. Like yeah, there's a cool little town. You could keep a cabin here if you must, and come up for weekends. But why are you torturing yourself with the long drive into the city? I'm dreading the trip back already."

Amanda didn't know how to respond to him. If he didn't like the island, she couldn't make him like it. He was entitled to his opinion.

It was just that...she had thought that maybe, if he saw the beaches and the beautiful views, and let himself be swept up in the charm of the little towns...

Then what? That he'd fall in love with the island, and in love with her again? That he'd tell her he'd been aching and missing her all this time?

No. Instead, she felt like she had to defend her love of this place. As Amanda watched his scowl set in, she realized that it would be a mistake to bring anything up about their relationship. He was not in a whimsical or sentimental mood.

"I'm sorry, Rupert. I know people who fly in – you know, from Seattle. My uncle used to fly planes."

"How long does that take?"

She shrugged. "About an hour."

"That's more bearable," he said. "Maybe I'll try that next time."

"Yeah. Maybe next time."

She should have felt grateful that he was talking about a next time, but somehow she just felt...flat.

Chapter 21

The coffee at this cafe was disgusting. Mike leaned back in his chair, shooting a glance at the front door. Still no sign of Amanda.

Maybe he was getting too used to Starbucks? He'd tried a new latte that week – something with pecan, toffee and whipped cream. Mike fully expected that it'd be terrible, but he was wrong. Starbucks had done it again. The latte was delicious, and he'd had four of them since. He'd always had a sweet tooth – just like his mom and his sister. He and his sister had more in common than she probably realized.

Mike had yet to tell Margie about his retirement, though; maybe now was the time? He was hoping that he wouldn't need to involve her in his ongoing investigation – or anyone else, for that matter. But Amanda's repeated interactions with the Dirk Gold Group employee meant that she was already involved.

He peeked at his watch – just a bit after noon. Maybe he'd missed Amanda again? Maybe she'd gone to a different restaurant?

Just then, the door opened and she walked through, head down and eyes on her phone. Mike watched as she stood in line, placed an order, and then waited just a few feet from his table.

"Excuse me, Miss?" Mike said softly, setting down his newspaper.

She didn't flinch. She stood there, scrolling through her phone and skillfully ignoring him.

He smiled. He was sure that she'd heard him.

"Miss? You dropped your taser."

She turned around, mouth open. "I'm sorry?"

He smiled, lifting his baseball cap slightly. "Hello Amanda."

"Mike?" She looked over her shoulder, then back at him. "Sorry, I hardly recognized you with that hat and weird facial hair."

He nodded. He wasn't particularly happy with how his beard had grown out, but it did the job. "That was kind of the point. Can I walk you back to your office?"

"Sure – I guess."

Her order was up. Amanda grabbed the bag and headed for the front door; Mike followed.

Once they were outside, she started pelting him with questions.

"How did you know where I was?"

"I've been keeping an eye on you."

"Oh. Am I in danger?"

"I don't think so, no. You really seem to like that restaurant. What is it that you keep ordering – the caprese?"

"Wow, you really *have* been stalking me. But your intel is off."

He smiled. "Is it?"

"I don't like the sandwich. My boss does – she sends me out to get it for her, almost every time she sees me. I'm getting really sick of it."

"Wow." He let out a whistle. "That's a far walk for lunch."

"You're telling me. How long have you been in Seattle?"

"A few weeks." He paused. Should he tell her that he'd had no trouble following her for the past two weeks? She was incredibly easy to track. It would probably just scare her. Better not to mention it.

"And...have you found anything interesting?"

"Sure. I've been trying to figure out what Lenny is up to."

"Ah. Well, all I know is that he owns some properties on San Juan Island, and DGG is buying them from him."

Mike nodded. "Right. That's what your friend is working on?"

She stopped and looked at him. "What do you know about Will?"

"Nothing really. I was hoping you could tell me some things."

She started walking again. "Nope. I mean, I don't know anything."

"How was the ball?" Mike asked.

Amanda groaned. "You followed me there, too?"

"No, I saw the pictures on the company website. If I'd have known that you were going, I would've stopped you. That was really dangerous, Lenny could have – "

"I know. I saw Lenny and I got out of there as fast as I could. I'm not even sure when they got a picture of me."

"That's the problem with those events," Mike said. "People go to be seen and then...there are lots of eyes to see them."

"I didn't stay very long."

Lenny saw her, but there was no use in belaboring his point. "That's good. And your friend?"

"Will." She let out a sigh. "I don't think that he knows what kind of business Lenny comes from."

Mike raised an eyebrow. "What makes you say that?"

"Because he took me to see this ridiculous property that obviously looked like the site of a mob movie."

"That doesn't mean anything."

"Well, and then I told him that one of his clients is in the mob and he was shocked. He didn't believe me."

Terrific. "Amanda. You shouldn't trust this guy, no matter how good of an act he puts on. Of course he knows. He must. If he doesn't, his boss does. You could be putting yourself in danger."

"Will isn't going to rat me out. He didn't even believe me. He thought I was making it up to push him away."

Mike sighed. This is what it was like to work with non-professionals. Though professionals got sloppy, too. "You're not worried about him wondering how you got this information?"

She waved a hand. "My dad's a cop. It's a *very* believable cover story. I didn't give him any details, or who it was, I just – accused him of working with the mob. Which he is!"

Oh boy. Maybe it was a mistake to involve Amanda at all. She was behaving...irrationally. What he should have done was emailed her back right away and told her to stay away from Lenny, DGG, and this Will character. But at the same time, her inside knowledge was useful.

"Do you think that you could get on to Will's computer?"

"Yeah. Probably. Why?"

"Because I've tried to get on to Lenny's computer and have been unsuccessful. But maybe there's information that your friend Will has access to, and – "

"Absolutely not. I'm not going to be involved in this anymore. Will stopped speaking to me, and that's for the best."

He nodded. "All right, never mind about that then. What about the properties? Did Will show them to you? Do you have access to them?"

"No. And I don't want access." Amanda stopped and turned toward him. "Listen, I appreciate that you care about this, and I thought I did too. But I can't be involved in it anymore. I'm sorry. I should have just let you know that I saw Lenny and left it at that, but I had to get nosy. Now I really regret it."

"Did something happen?"

She shook her head. "No. Just the whole...thing with Will."

Oh. Mike frowned. *That's* why she was behaving strangely. There seemed to be some feelings involved here. He'd missed her earlier cues – emotions and romance were not his strong suit. In fact, there might not be anyone less qualified to offer advice to a young woman on her love life. Time to change the subject. "I understand. Well – I appreciate the tip. I'll stay out of your way."

"Thank you."

"Just one more thing – before you go. Do you recognize anyone in these pictures? They're some of Lenny's associates."

They stopped, moving to the edge of the sidewalk as people walked by. He handed her his cell phone, open to the pictures he'd managed to snap.

To any bystander, it would look like they were exchanging numbers or showing off family pictures – not that anyone was watching. Or at least, he didn't have any reason to think that they were.

Amanda flipped through the pictures, frowning and pausing at one. "I know that guy. That's Jared."

Mike leaned in to see who she was pointing at – a guy he'd photographed meeting with Lenny last week. "Jared who?"

"Jared Knape. He used to be on the San Juan County Council. He's the one who burned Jade's house down when she first started trying to build the new state park."

"I see. Interesting. Very interesting."

She handed the phone back. "I'm sorry, I don't know anyone else. But good luck with everything."

He nodded. He wanted to say something comforting to her about whatever she was going through romantically, but since he wasn't even comfortable hearing about it, he couldn't craft anything appropriate. "Thanks. Stay safe."

He watched as she disappeared into the crowd, then spotted a Starbucks across the street.

Perfect. He tossed the coffee from the cafe into the trash – he'd barely had any of it. It was time to get back to his favorite pecan toffee surprise. And to look into this Jared individual.

Chapter 22

One of the landscapers that Amanda recommended ended up being a delight to work with; Will spent the week directing his crew on the new estate and was impressed with their progress.

He appreciated that Amanda still sent him the recommendations after their spat, but he wasn't going to keep trying to be her friend. Clearly she wanted to push him away badly enough to weave this lie about mob activity on the island.

Ridiculous. It was one thing if she disapproved of his efforts to make money off of the properties here. And it was still another thing if she was in a quasi-relationship with her long-lost ex-boyfriend.

Sure, whatever. That was all fine and he was happy leaving her alone.

Yet she still wasn't satisfied. It wasn't until she casually told him that he was probably working with the mob that he snapped. Was it her way of signaling that she thought he was sleazy? Or was it just an extension of her self-destructive streak – setting off bombs around anything even resembling a new relationship?

Will wasn't sure, and he didn't have much time to think about it. Gordon wanted to get the new estate up and running by the summer. Will spent his days on the property, directing contractors, plumbers, landscapers, electricians – everyone that they needed to get this place out of disarray.

They already had building plans completed from their staff architect, and an engineer had cleared all of the structures. They were paying a premium to get the estate in shape as soon as possible, so it'd be ready for the busy summer season of tourists.

Later that week, Gordon called to check in on the progress. Will gave him a full update and promised to tweak the timeline, and to create a report to share with investors. Gordon was trying to rush him off of the phone when Will stuck in one more question.

"Last thing – have you talked to Lenny recently? I know that we closed on a few of his properties, but I didn't know when you wanted me to start working on them."

"Don't go near those properties. Not for a while."

Will frowned. "Ah, okay. No problem. It's just that he's my biggest client so I want to make sure – "

"Yeah, yeah. Do me a favor, and stay out of it."

"Okay." He paused. "And the properties he's holding onto? The rentals? Should I start planning renovations for them, or are – "

"What part of 'stay out of it' do you not get, Will?"

"Uh…" Will cleared his throat. "I just want to make sure that our biggest client is happy."

"He's happy. He's fine. You're killing me, though. Get back to work Will."

After they ended the phone call, Will told himself to focus on the work at the estate. He told himself that the way his boss acted about Lenny wasn't weird, and that it couldn't possibly have anything to do with what Amanda had said.

He also told himself that he was misremembering that framed mugshot that Amanda had in her house. At the time he thought it looked vaguely like Lenny, and since then he could only remember it *as* Lenny. But it must've been his imagination warping an unfortunate doppelganger – Lenny wasn't a unique looking guy. He was so average that he was almost a caricature. It just so happened that he looked like the caricature of...a criminal.

He repeated these things to himself over and over again, but didn't get any closer to believing them. That Saturday, he decided to take a break from the estate to go and look at one of the apartment buildings that they were supposed to eventually manage for Lenny.

No, he wasn't supposed to and he felt silly doing it, but he couldn't stop thinking about it. He reasoned that DGG would soon be getting a cut of the rent and he needed to see what work needed to be done; it had nothing to do with suppressing the uneasy feeling in his chest.

The complex was on the edge of Friday Harbor. It was a bit off the beaten track, but still walkable from town. When Will pulled up, he was impressed by the size of the place – it was a five story high brick building, its horseshoe-shaped walls wrapping around much of the block. Granted, it wasn't a huge block, but it was the only building like it that he'd seen on the island.

There was a garden and common area out front. There wasn't much foliage – he noticed these things now – but the grass looked healthy enough. Will pulled around the back of the building and was surprised to see that there weren't any cars parked in the expansive lot – except for one broken down Buick that looked like it'd been there for ages. The tires were flat and one of the windows was taped up.

"That's odd..."

He pulled out the file he had on this property. It had originally been built in 1982 and had over thirty luxury apartments, according to his records. There were a range of sizes – from studios and one bedrooms, to multi-level apartments and lofts. All told, the building had a gross revenue of three million dollars in rent per year.

Will paused. The math there didn't add up. How much were they charging for the apartments every month? Certainly they weren't getting an average of eight *thousand* dollars a month for each of these apartments?

He leaned forward and peered around. And if they were, who were these people? How much was a parking spot? Were they paying a few thousand a month to park here or something? That would be an oddity for the island.

The company Lenny represented, Sun Kissing Holdings, claimed that this apartment building was worth thirty *million* dollars, citing that there was an expected growth in rent.

Will ran through the numbers again. None of this made any sense. How could this apartment building, even with wealthy clients, be worth *that* much more than even the extravagant estate?

Will ignored the squeezing in his stomach – it must've been something he'd eaten. Yeah, maybe that questionable cheese from yesterday. And not the fear that he was about to walk into a drug trafficking den.

His decision was made, though. He got out of the car.

There didn't seem to be anyone around; maybe somebody would let him in if he pretended to have a friend in the building? If there was a doorman, though, he'd bail.

He got to the front door – no doorman – and was surprised to see that the door to the lobby looked damaged. He tugged on the handle and realized that his suspicions were correct – the lock was broken and it opened easily.

Will walked into the lobby, unimpressed by what he saw. It resembled an old movie theater – red carpets, large mirrors on the wall, and a musty smell, as if the place had gotten wet and dried several dozen times.

Still no one around. He breezed through the lobby and down one of the hallways. The first two doors were unlabeled, but he did find a number "1" lying on the ground next to the stairwell. So one of these doors led to an apartment, apparently.

He didn't dare try to open any doors; many of the edges were dinged, as though someone had tried to kick them open. He stood still and listened for signs of life – a TV, someone coughing, anything.

But there was nothing.

What the heck? This place was completely run down. It looked worse than the estate. Will walked over to the elevator and pressed the button – maybe the upper floors were nicer?

It took a few moments for the elevator to arrive, and when it did, the doors were barely able to open. The left door was off kilter, dragging a corner along the ground and making a squeal as it did. He popped his head into the elevator and quickly pulled away – the smell of urine was overwhelming.

Was that raccoon urine...or human?

He started coughing and instead decided to head up the stairs. He made the mistake of holding onto the banister which was wobbly and gave way, throwing him off balance.

This couldn't be right, this couldn't *possibly* be right. He must've gone to the wrong place.

He got to the second floor and saw that the doors here were at least numbered, so that was good. He couldn't stop coughing; the smell of urine seemed to follow him.

One of the apartment doors flew open and he found himself face to face with a woman.

"Can I help you?" she said, hands on her hips.

"Oh, I'm looking for my friend...Carl?"

She looked him up and down. "There's no Carl here. Who're you?"

How could she possibly know that there was no Carl in the entire building? It didn't matter. "I must have the wrong address, I'm sorry."

He rushed down the stairs, not looking back as he ran through the stinking lobby and out the front doors, back to his car, and away from this place.

When he'd gotten a few blocks away, he parked his car and pulled out the folder again.

Yes – he'd definitely had the right address. But the picture of the building looked entirely different. It looked like a digital rendering, actually. As did all of the indoor shots.

Sometimes they used a computer program to fill empty houses with furniture, just to make them look more homey. He was used to seeing it, and it didn't strike him as odd at first.

However now, the closer he looked at the pictures, the more he realized that they all looked fake. Everything about them looked fake, not just the furniture.

Was that why Lenny didn't want him in the building? Because it was a dud and he didn't think anyone would notice?

Will pulled out his phone and called his boss.

"Will, my man, how's it going?"

"Not so good."

"Don't tell me that you have bad news for me."

He sighed. "I think I do. Really bad news. I just went out to the apartment building that we're supposed to rent out from Sun Kissing Holdings. You know – the one worth thirty million?"

"Yeah..."

"The place is a total dump, Gordon. Lenny kept telling me that they had people living there and that they were working on it, but that was a lie. The lobby is in shambles, it smells like raccoons peed on everything, and I could see water damage on the ceilings and on the walls. It's in really poor shape."

"Don't worry about that. We can fix it."

"But that's the thing – what kind of investment is this? I didn't go into any of the units, but there's no way that they look anything like the pictures they gave us. Who did the walk-through on this? Do we have someone on our team who has Lenny's best interests at heart instead of ours?"

"I said don't worry about it." Gordon said firmly. "If you can't handle a challenge, then I'll find someone who will."

"I can handle it, of course I can handle it," Will said quickly. "I'm just thinking that – "

"Stop thinking. I don't pay you to think, I pay you to work. Quit being an idiot, Will. Don't call me about this again."

Out of all of the arguments he'd had with his boss in the past, he'd never before felt like they weren't talking about the same thing.

How many millions would they need to sink into that building to make it livable again? There was no way they were pulling in millions a year for rent – there weren't even people living there, except that one angry lady!

There was just no way that the sale made sense. Maybe if they bulldozed it and built a brand new building? But then what was the point of planning to invest in the property? Was it a zoning thing? Had his boss gotten the wool pulled over his eyes and now he was too ashamed to back down?

Worst of all, their team was already stretched to the limit working on the other properties, particularly the estate. It could be months before they even got into this building.

He didn't think that Amanda was right – it didn't look like there was any sort of mob activity going on at the building. It was just a piece of junk. Will didn't know what to make of it.

His phone rang – the landscaper. "Hello?"

"Hey, we pulled up a patch of bushes and found some kind of a stone patio. Flagstone, I think. You probably want to check it out – decide if it's something that we need to keep or redo."

"I'll be right there."

The apartment building wasn't his problem – at least not for now. He needed to focus on the work he had; that was what they were paying him for.

Chapter 23

After skipping work on Monday, Amanda fell behind at work. It was predictable, and she reasoned that that was why she felt tired all week, but something else was bugging her, too. She couldn't put her finger on it, but she felt...off.

Rupert had noticed and bought her a scone on Friday to cheer her up. It was nice of him, but also made her realize she must've really been sulking if even Rupert took note.

She didn't feel like she had a moment to herself until the weekend. For once, she didn't have to wait around wondering if Rupert was going to visit. He'd already made up an excuse as to why he couldn't come, and she didn't ask questions. He clearly hadn't enjoyed his first visit, and she didn't expect him to come again soon.

It was embarrassing for them both that he had to pretend to have an excuse – in the future, she'd tell him that there was no expectation on him, and that he didn't need to worry about making something up. She could handle the truth – he didn't like the island. Oh well.

That Sunday began, like many before it, with Morgan's voice rousing her from sleep. Amanda opened her eyes when she heard Morgan's screams from the front door.

Amanda awoke and, shuffling like a zombie, went to see what the commotion was. She found Morgan halfway outside, yelling after a family of deer.

"Get out of here, you hoofed assassins! You are *not* welcome!"

Amanda rubbed her eyes, standing behind her. "Fighting with the woodland creatures again?"

"Only because they eat *everything* that isn't nailed down!" Morgan waved her hands menacingly.

The deer stared at her, unmoved.

Amanda put a hand on her shoulder. "How about you come back inside."

She glared a bit too long before responding, "Fine."

Once the door was shut, Amanda got the full story. Morgan had gotten an azalea from Luke as a gift before he'd left. She was worried that it wasn't getting enough sunlight, so yesterday, she made the decision to give it an outdoor trip. Unfortunately, she forgot to bring it in overnight, much to the deer's delight.

"There's nothing left," Morgan said, pointing at the ravaged flower pot.

"I'm sorry, I know that you miss Luke."

"Miss him?" Morgan laughed. "It's not about that! Luke is going to make fun of me *so bad*. The deer ate the *one* thing that he told me to take care of until he came back!"

"Oh. Right." Amanda tried not to laugh. "Well, I know it's not the same, but let me get you another one. Luke won't know the difference."

It was a good excuse to get herself out of the house. She knew of a farm in the middle of the island – it was a large property with greenhouses, a nursery, orchards, and rolling lavender fields. Her mom used to be friends with the owners, Sue and Paul. They were a lovely couple who'd lived on the island for years, and sold fruit from the orchards at the farmer's market. When her mom passed away, Sue and Paul came to the funeral with the most beautiful and elaborate flower arrangement that Amanda had ever seen.

That day had been a blur to her, but their kindness shined through. Amanda felt guilty that she hadn't been over to see them since.

She pulled out her computer and checked the website – it looked like the farm was alive and well, and Sue and Paul were still in charge. They had Sunday hours and invited people to browse the plants and walk the gardens.

That would be perfect. Amanda would replace Morgan's plant and say hello to some old friends.

Yet as she was getting ready, she started to feel more and more nostalgic. Her mom had loved gardening, and had kept the landscaping around their house in much better shape than it was now. She'd be disappointed to see its current state.

A memory floated in and Amanda laughed to herself – one time when she got into a fight with her mom during high school, she was forced to go to the nursery and pick up flowers for a new backyard bed. She then had to weed the garden and plant the flowers, but in an act of spiteful teenage behavior, she purposely didn't plant the roots deep enough.

Somehow it didn't matter, and they bloomed marvelously. She remembered it like it was yesterday, walking up and down the greenhouse with her mom, arms crossed, and not speaking. They'd gotten into the fight because Amanda was out past curfew, and after she was caught, a screaming match began. Amanda remembered her mom telling her that she was being an ungrateful brat.

Ha. Not untrue.

They hadn't always gotten along in those years. In fact, there was a lot of yelling. It made Amanda cringe now to think of it. After she went off to college, their relationship substantially improved. But Amanda had been a difficult teenager; she could see that now. *How* had her mom put up with her?

Worse, how could Amanda have taken her mom for granted like that? Why did she assume that they would have forever to make up?

For some reason, it was really on her mind today. She expected to feel this way on anniversaries – her mom's birthday, the day of her mom's death – things like that. Mother's Day was never easy, but the other days never hit her as hard as she expected.

It seemed that grief didn't play by any rules. On random days, memories rolled in like dark clouds, disturbing the peace with bouts of wind, rain and hail, all along with periodic flashes of sun. Grief was exhausting.

It'd be good to get out of the house and get out of her head. Amanda got into her car and drove to the farm, surprised to see that it was quite busy.

She felt suddenly nervous about seeing Sue and Paul again. They were probably busy helping customers; they didn't have time to catch up. Or worse – what if they really *wanted* to catch up and Amanda did something inappropriate like burst into tears? She wasn't usually one to cry, but the day had her on edge.

She avoided the bustling greenhouses and instead turned to walk through the empty lavender fields. The plants were all dead now, as it was winter – or maybe not dead, but dormant? Amanda wasn't sure. She never did get very interested in plants.

The lavender bushes still stood cheerful and wide, but their leaves were gray and stiff. She bent down to get a closer look. Were they dead? Or were they just...waiting?

Amanda couldn't really tell, but it was peaceful to walk up and down the fields. She admired the way the lavender rows flowed ever so gently with the rolling hills in the distance. In the summer, the lavender would surely come back to life, rows and rows of the purple flowers all coming together and swaying like a dream.

Her mom had loved lavender. She grew it along the walkway to the house. That was one plant that survived with little maintenance – the lavender came back year after year.

Amanda's footsteps felt heavy; she must not have slept well. She decided to take a break and sit down in the dirt. The ground was colder than she expected, and it felt like it was draining the heat and the life from her body.

She didn't care.

She sat there and thought of all the times she'd come here with her mother, annoyed that she had to spend a weekend pulling weeds or digging up grass to make more room for flowerbeds. Amanda had hated everything about gardening. She hated wearing a big hat, she hated the way that her hands got sweaty inside the gloves and how they stung. She hated the bugs that emerged from the soil and surprised her, making her scream. She only did it because her mom made her do it, and now she was looking back on gardening as one of her fondest memories.

That was all she had now. The memories. She'd never get to make more memories with her mom. She'd never get to walk these fields together again, annoyed by whatever escapade they were on, or by whatever disagreement they'd had.

Surely, if she were still alive, they'd be annoying each other with some regularity – but in a good way. A loving way. Amanda might've casually complained to her friends about her mom wanting her to come home and visit, or she might've had to tell her mom to take it easy on her new boyfriend. She laughed to herself – what would her mom have thought of Rupert?

Unlike her dad, her mom was able to keep her opinions to herself. She might not say anything at all, though she likely wouldn't have liked him proudly announcing that he wasn't "the marrying type."

Would Amanda *ever* get married? Would any guy want to commit to a life sentence with her?

It didn't matter – her mom would never meet him anyway. She buried her head in her hands as all the silly feelings came spilling out. The emotions caught in her throat and she let out a sob – first one, quietly, then more, until she was flat-out crying, like a loon. Luckily, there was no one but the lavender to witness her breakdown.

Until, of course, she heard a voice from behind her. "Amanda?"

She thought she was imagining it. She looked up, hurriedly wiping the tears from her face, but no one was there.

"Are you okay?" said the voice.

Amanda stood up to see Will standing behind her in the next row of lavender. At first she thought that she was imagining him, but there he was. The real Will, with the dead plants blowing in the breeze between them.

"Hi, how are you?" she said, trying to recover the quiver from her voice.

"I'm fine, but are you okay?"

Her hips were stiff from standing up so quickly; how long had she been sitting in the cold dirt? "Yeah, great. Everything is great."

"I came by the nursery for my landscaper – your recommendation, by the way. Thank you again for that, he's great."

"You're welcome, glad that it's working out."

"And I thought I saw – well, something bobbing around out here, I thought it was a loose dog."

She looked around. There was no one else. "Oh, ah – maybe I missed him. A big dog?"

He looked down then back up at her. "Are you – "

She sighed. It was nice of him to try, but the dog ruse didn't make sense. "I used to come here a lot. With my mom. She loved flowers." Amanda laughed at herself. What a bizarre statement to make. But then again, what a bizarre situation to find herself in.

"Oh yeah?"

She nodded. "I used to fight with her so much about gardening when I was in high school. I hated it. I still do. But she loved this place. She loved the lavender. Have you thought about putting lavender on the estate? It's a very San Juan Island sort of thing."

He smiled. "I haven't, actually. Hang on a sec."

She nodded dumbly, watching as he walked off toward the greenhouse.

Amanda could've kicked herself. What was the matter with her? Why had she come to this stupid field? Of all the places that Will could find her having an emotional breakdown, it had to be here.

She kept telling herself to pull it together and to stop thinking about her mom, but the more she told herself not to do it, the more she felt like she was going to go over the edge. It felt like she was balancing a stack of plates in each hand, and the earth was quaking beneath her feet.

Will returned a few minutes later with a blanket and a thermos. "You look cold. I was planning to spend the day at the estate, so I've got all of this coffee. Would you like some?"

"Sure," was all she managed to say.

He spread the blanket out on the ground and she took a seat. It was much more comfortable than before. She sat in silence as he poured coffee into the lid of the thermos and handed it to her.

"Thanks."

After a moment, he asked, "I know you said your mom passed away...was it recently?"

Amanda shook her head. "No. It's been...four years."

She took a sip of the coffee, trying to maintain her composure, but it was no use. The harder she tried and the nicer he was, the more impossible it became. Tears slid down her cheeks.

"I'm so sorry, I'm just a mess today, I don't know what's gotten into me."

"It's okay," he said. After a moment, he continued. "What was she like? Your mom."

Amanda took a deep breath and smiled. "She was funny, in a goofy kind of way. She liked to sing and dance, she liked being outside, and always read to us when we were kids. And she'd go fishing with my dad, even though she hated it." Amanda laughed. Her mom *really* hated it, and her dad would always scold her for talking too much and scaring away all of the fish.

Will kept looking at her, and she kept talking. It was pouring out – the Friday nights at the deli shop after football games. The time that Amanda cut her own hair, and it looked like a disaster, and then her mom tried to fix it and only made it worse. The grounding she got after being caught sneaking out of her window. The camping trips they used to take to Posey Island. The trips to the mainland with her parents when she was little, and they'd go to the mall and she threw coins into the fountain.

Then she told him about the rest of it. The cancer. The way that her dad shut down after her mom's death. How Amanda ran away – clear over to London, and how she stayed away as long as she could. How mean she was to Margie. The guilt. The regrets. The reality that there was no chance for her to apologize, or to have one more good day together, even if it was gardening. The fact that all of her memories from now on were all that she would have.

Will listened to all of it, quietly filling her coffee whenever it got low.

"So – yeah. That's just a little bit about me," Amanda said with a laugh.

Will smiled. "How long have you been holding that in?"

"Oh, I don't know..." She shrugged. "Just a few years."

He offered her a pained smile.

She continued. "I'm desperate to hang onto these memories of her, even the bad ones. Not that they're bad – they were just everyday things. But I feel them all slipping away. I just can't...I can't live without them."

Will was quiet for a moment. He pulled a sprig from a nearby lavender plant and picked the dried leaves off, one by one. "You shouldn't feel guilty about the 'bad' memories. Your relationship with your mom evolved over the years – and it sounds like at the end, things were really good."

Amanda shrugged. "They were. But I was so nasty as a teenager. Such a brat. It's kind of all blurring together now."

"I'm sure your mom didn't see it that way. Your relationship with her is continuing to evolve. You're not in that acute grief phase anymore. In some ways it's bad, because the memories get further away."

"Yeah." Amanda nodded. Had she expressed herself better this time, or had Rupert just been dense when she tried to tell him?

"And in other ways, you're able to see things with less pain. You were able to stop being mean to your dad's new wife, so that's pretty good."

She sputtered out a laugh. "That's true."

"With all of the stories that you told me – it sounds like you remember what your mom taught you. Even if you didn't like all of the lessons, like with the gardening. You grew up because of the gardening. And you're not going to lose that, or lose her. How could you?"

Her eyes filled with tears again, and she kept her head down. He was right, of course. "I just wish things could be different."

"Yeah. I know."

Amanda wanted to say something, apologize for being so harsh about Lenny and the mob. She wasn't sure exactly *what* to say, but she had to try.

"Listen, about – "

And his phone rang. Of course.

"Oh, don't mind me, you should answer."

He smiled, and had a quick conversation before hanging up. "Sorry about that. My landscaper asked if I fell into a well."

She laughed. "Sorry, I didn't mean to monopolize your time with my babbling. You should get back to it."

"It wasn't babbling," he said. "I like talking to you."

What else was there to say? The man needed to get back to work. She stood up and dusted off her pants. "Thanks a lot for this, Will. I...really appreciate it."

"Any time."

Amanda folded up the blanket and handed it to him. Should she suggest that they hang out again? Maybe she could get him fish and chips as a thank you?

She'd figure it out later, he needed to get going.

"Good luck with the estate!" she said, forcing a smile.

"Ah – thanks. Take care."

She watched him disappear before walking into the greenhouse to find Sue and Paul. She felt lighter than she had in weeks. Normally, she would've felt embarrassed for crying in front of someone – especially someone like Will. But she didn't feel embarrassed at all.

Something within her had snapped. All that crying served a purpose, it seemed. There'd been a leak in the dam; and now, it was fully cracked open.

Chapter 24

Once he was back in his car, Will hesitated. What did he care about the landscaping? He should tell them to plant whatever they wanted to, and that was that.

He'd much rather spend his day with Amanda. Maybe he should go back and find her? Tell her that he was free for the rest of the day? It was a weekend, after all. They could surely get by without him at the estate.

At the same time, he didn't want to spoil the moment. Though she'd been sharing her past quite freely, it was clear that she was done. Amanda literally packed it up; she'd folded up his blanket, handed it back, and got up to leave.

He'd seen glimpses of her opening up before, but this was the first time that she'd let him in. He didn't know what had caused it, exactly, but he wasn't going to ask questions. By some miracle of the universe, he happened to walk onto that farm at precisely the right moment.

Will let out a sigh. It was best to leave her alone for now. He'd made that mistake in the past – he didn't want to scare her off again. She might have to come up with something even more outlandish to push him away – that she thought Gordon was a martian, or something.

Actually, the more that he thought about her mafia theory, the more uncomfortable he became. It wasn't just that the apartment building was a dump – that wasn't a *huge* surprise. It was how Gordon reacted when he asked about it. He got defensive; he got mean. Though Gordon was mean with a regular frequency, it usually didn't bother Will. This time felt different.

Will got back to the estate and clarified some issues about the grass near the gate, as well as a thorny overgrowth on the beach. The plumber approached him with questions about the new toilets, and Will told him he'd be up in a minute.

He wanted to send a message to Amanda first – he had a doorway back into their friendship, and he didn't want to mess it up.

"Hey – it was really nice running into you today. I swear that I'm not stalking you, I know how you get about that."

He paused. Maybe he *shouldn't* bring up stalking? She'd accused him of following her onto the ferry that first day, which he still thought was funny – but she might not remember that. She might just decide that he *was* a stalker.

He deleted the stalking line and instead wrote, "I'm sorry about our argument. I'm starting to believe you, because things aren't quite right around here. Maybe we could chat about it this week? Get dinner?"

Much to his relief, she responded about an hour later. "I'm sorry, too. Honestly, you'd be better off ditching DGG. I know that's not a great option. I can't tell you much else. But I'd love to get dinner – I owe you fish and chips for all that blubbering. Are you free this week?"

He smiled. He appreciated the pun – blubbering and fish. Was that intentional? Probably – Amanda was always cracking him up with things like that. He suggested Friday for dinner; he hoped she'd be less rushed on a Friday evening.

"Friday it is," she wrote back. "That's actually perfect. Gives me time to take care of some things."

Hm. That sounded ominous. Did she mean with work?

Or was Amanda...involved with something shadier? Something more...illegal? Is that what she'd meant before when she said they shouldn't spend time together?

No. It must've been something with her regular, non-mafia related job.

And if things went well on Friday, maybe they could make plans again on Saturday. And on Sunday. And on every day after that.

Until then, though, he had to keep working. Monday and Tuesday were eaten up with issues on the estate. But on Wednesday, Will decided that it was time to investigate the rest of Lenny's properties. He had two hours free in the afternoon and decided to take a little trip around the island.

The first property was described as "an idyllic cabin on the water."

What he found when he got there was a hastily slapped together shed, its walls collapsing inward, and the roof spattered with holes. It sat on an acre of land, which was nice, but it was not worth the two million dollars that DGG had already paid for it.

Next up was a condo on the outskirts of town. It was run down, and Will mistakenly assumed that it was also uninhabitable. He found his mistake when he knocked on the door and a disgruntled man in a robe asked him, "Who do you think you are barging in here like this?" Will apologized and pretended that he had the wrong address.

The third property sat on five acres of land, and was described as "a peaceful, farm-like setting for camping and unwinding." DGG paid six million for it, and it boasted "ample room for camping, glamping, and recreational fun."

At this point, Will shouldn't have been surprised to find a dump, but this place was *actually* a dump. He counted three broken down cars on the property. There weren't any cabins like the description said – there was one trailer, which looked even more run down than the shed he'd seen before, and what appeared to be the remnants of a tent. He almost fell into a partially buried bathtub – full of rainwater and muck.

This wasn't right – *none* of this was right. He didn't know how deeply involved his boss was, but now Will knew and he couldn't pretend to be ignorant. He didn't know if Lenny was involved in the mafia – there was no evidence to suggest that – but something fishy was going on.

He stood around the dump for thirty minutes, trying to decide his next move. He wasn't sure how much he could accomplish on his own; Will still wasn't a partner and was still a lowly employee in the company.

But the shareholders deserved to know what their money was being wasted on – and that was part of his job description, preparing reports. Did Gordon expect that when the time came, Will would forge the reports? That he'd not mention the collapsing structures, the cars and the outdoor bathtubs?

He needed to get back to the estate for now, but tomorrow, he'd get his good camera and take pictures of the properties. It might cost him his job at DGG, but he didn't care.

He'd worked his way up once, and he could do it again. Whatever was going on here needed to be unveiled. Amanda was right – if this sort of behavior was allowed, then DGG wasn't a place that he wanted to work.

With a spring in his step, Will walked back to his car. Maybe by Friday he'd have some good news to share with Amanda.

Chapter 25

"The kid did *what*?"

Lenny frowned as he listened. His little buddy, Will, had showed up, uninvited, at three of the properties on San Juan Island.

Lenny had told Gordon that he needed someone with discretion for these places. And Gordon should have known better – this was a delicate business that needed to be handled quietly. Benzini didn't like nosy bystanders.

Each of the properties needed to be handled by someone who wasn't counting pennies – better yet, someone who couldn't count at all.

He'd suspected that this Will kid was too smart for all of it – a liability. What was he doing, peeking into windows and knocking on doors? Lenny had *specifically* told him on *multiple* occasions not to go poking around!

And what did he do? Go poke around!

Lenny was sick of hearing about it. "I'm on it. Thanks."

He hung up the phone. He wasn't going to let this kid screw things up for him. Lenny had wasted so much time on that stupid island, forced to watch as that idiotic zombie movie fell apart. Yeah, it was Benzini's son, it was important to keep the kid happy. But it was like a babysitting job. A joke.

Now he was *finally* getting the respect that he deserved – all while bringing in millions of dollars – and some kid with a calculator was going to start pointing out that things weren't adding up?

No way.

He called Gordon, who picked up right away. At least he knew his place.

"If it isn't my favorite client!" Gordon said.

"Hey, I warned you. I told you to keep that kid out of the way."

"Whoa whoa, Lenny, what's going on? I'm sure it's just a misunderstanding."

"It's not a misunderstanding. He went to the apartments last week, and today he went to each and every property. We have him on camera. Is he still asking questions?"

"No, nothing, he just expressed some concerns that we're going to need more resources. You know, to bring the properties up to par. That's his job, Lenny. Will's a good kid, he's not going to cause any trouble."

"You're right that he won't. Because he's done."

"What's that supposed to mean? Come on Lenny, don't be hasty. We need the kid in one piece – he's doing great work out there – he's a real go-getter. That's all, he's just a go-getter."

"Not once I'm done with him."

Lenny ended the call and was about to make another when the barista waved him over.

"Hi sir, are you ready?"

The call could wait a minute. He'd been standing in line for this coffee for ages. He didn't want anyone getting ahead of him.

Lenny stepped up. "Thank you Miss. And might I say, what lovely eyes you have."

She smiled.

She probably *never* got complemented – not many guys were as confident as he was.

"How can I help you?"

He wanted one of those milkshake frappuccino-type things, but he couldn't order something like that from such a pretty thing. That wouldn't impress her. It wasn't manly. And this Starbucks was only a block from his place, so he'd be seeing a lot of her. First impressions were so important. "I'll take a large black coffee."

"Will that be all?"

He nodded. He'd have to stick to ordering the fancy drinks at a different Starbucks. "That'll be all. Thanks beautiful."

He stepped aside to wait for his coffee and pulled out his phone. "Hey, I'm gonna need a plane. To San Juan Island. Now."

Chapter 26

After seeing Will in the lavender field, it took Amanda a few days to figure out exactly how she felt. She felt better, *so much better*, but she wasn't sure exactly why.

Eventually, she realized it was because her stories didn't annoy Will, and he didn't think that they were worthless. Then, the thought hit her: *she* wasn't worthless. She was a worthwhile person, with a worthwhile history.

She'd had a mom who loved her, who had made her pancakes and braided her hair and read her stories. She'd run through the lavender fields, and laughed, and threw tantrums, and then made up. Amanda had lived a whole life, she was a whole person, with good and bad.

And even though she wasn't perfect, she was worth more than being Rupert's leftovers – she was worth more than his begrudging visits, his situational generosity, and his halfhearted attempts. She was worth more than her boss sending her out in the rain for sandwiches, and belittling her for how she looked.

From that moment on, everything became clear.

Her first order of business was dealing with Rupert. She was angry at herself for waiting around for him for *so long*. *Why* had she done it? How could she not have seen what he was really like?

He'd complained about the trip from Seattle to San Juan Island – a trip that he made *one* time, and that she'd made multiple times a week, just for the chance to get lunch together!

When Amanda allowed herself to think about her mom – and to talk about her mom – she laughed, realizing how much her mom would've hated Rupert. Instead of being paralyzed by her memories of the past, Amanda was now able to see her life through a different lens – through eyes that loved her. Her mom, who loved her so tenderly, would've despised the way that Rupert treated her.

All at once, Amanda knew that she needed to break up with him. It took her a while to get to the decision, but once made, she had no doubts about it. And it went...about as well as she'd expected. Which is to say, not that well.

Actually, there was no part of Wednesday that went according to plan. Initially, she wanted to break up with him in person. Amanda had never broken up with someone that she wasn't *technically* dating before, but she thought it was best to do it face-to-face.

Yet she nixed that idea quickly; it wasn't worth the trip or the trouble. And as if on cue that morning, Rupert sent her a message. "Hey babe, would you mind grabbing me a coffee on your way in? Hectic day, don't know if I can make lunch but I'd like to see you."

Amanda smiled. The old her – that is, the Amanda from a week ago – would've jumped on this proposal. She would've been sad that he couldn't make lunch, but she'd have wanted to see him, so despite her long commute into the city, she would've gotten that coffee for him.

She typed a message in response. "I'm not coming in today. Also, I don't think that we should see each other anymore. I wish you the best."

She debated adding more, but what else was there to say? She felt so freed by her revelation. She didn't need him – she didn't even remember what she liked about him. He was there right after her mom passed, yes – but he hadn't been there for her since. Her own muddled thoughts and feelings kept her trapped in his grips for *far* too long. But now she was free.

A few minutes after she sent the text, her phone rang. It was him.

"Hello?"

"All right, what're you playing at?"

"I'm not playing at anything. I've been doing some thinking, and...yeah. I don't think we should see each other anymore."

He sighed. "I knew you would do something like this. I knew that you would try to force some sort of ultimatum. You know that relationships aren't built on threats."

She rolled her eyes. To think that this used to work on her. "It's not a threat, Rupert. We don't have a relationship. It's just been me chasing you. Waiting around for you to grace me with your presence."

"There it is. You're bitter. You're bitter because I don't do things on your timeline."

She laughed. "I'm really not bitter. I don't have a timeline."

"Right, so if I told you that I wanted to get back together right now, you'd say no?"

"Yes."

He scoffed. "So you'd say yes?"

"No," she said slowly. "I was agreeing that I would say no to getting back together. I don't want to get back together. Not anymore."

"You know what Amanda, fine. Play your little games, see how far they get you."

"Goodbye Rupert."

Her heart leapt when she hung up the phone. She hadn't felt so free in – well, years! Even when she and Rupert were together, there was always an insecurity there, like he could pull away at any moment.

But not wanting that anymore, and not needing him? It was so liberating. Amanda felt like she could run out of the house, jump into Haro Strait and swim clear to Victoria.

Not that she was going to do that, of course. She had work to do, and her boss was annoyed that she'd changed her plans about coming into the office. Amanda didn't care – she was using the spare time that she would've used commuting to apply to new jobs.

Rupert tried calling once more, but Amanda didn't answer. Around noon, she got a call from an unknown number. Thinking that it might be a client, she answered it, only to find that it was Rupert. Again.

"Bet you didn't expect that," he said quickly.

"What? What are you talking about?"

He laughed. "There's another man, isn't there?"

Amanda wasn't sure how to answer that. Technically there *was* another man, even if the man in question didn't know it. "It doesn't matter, does it Rupert?"

"Of course it matters. I wouldn't have let you go out with other men if I knew that you were going to turn your back on me."

Now it was Amanda's turn to laugh. "*Let* me? You don't own me. And just because *you* didn't want to commit to me, doesn't mean that nobody does."

"Very smart, go ahead and just rush into a new relationship because I hurt your overly-sensitive feelings."

Amanda let out a sigh. She was wrong to assume that Rupert would let her go easily. It seemed he still liked her – or at least, he liked having power over her. "Okay Rupert. Good-bye again."

She set down her phone a little too hard. His comments stung, but when she took the time to examine them, his argument fell apart.

Silly Rupert seemed to think he had some claim on her – a right to keep her waiting around and hopeful. How was Jade able to see it so clearly before, while she'd totally missed it?

Jade was right, of course – Amanda had accepted that kind of treatment from him because she didn't think that she deserved better. She never spelled it out, but it was true. Her insecurities kept her questioning herself instead of questioning him – and her entire life suffered for it.

She managed to get back into work until a bit before three when her phone rang again. Amanda let out a dramatic sigh.

Another unknown number. She wasn't going to answer it if he was just going to berate her more.

The phone rang again and again – each time from a different number. How was he getting all of these numbers? Amanda silenced her phone, determined to ignore him.

She returned to work and after about ten minutes, Jade walked into her room.

"Hey, Amanda?"

She looked up from her laptop. "What's up?"

"I...have a phone call for you."

Amanda frowned. How had Rupert gotten Jade's phone number? "Are you serious? Tell him that he needs to cool down."

Jade raised an eyebrow. "Uh, Uncle Mike, are you still there?"

"Wait," Amanda held up a hand. "I thought it was Rupert, sorry."

"Rupert? No – it's my Uncle Mike. He said it's an emergency."

Amanda outstretched a hand. "Sorry about that, I'll take his call." She cleared her throat. "Mike?"

"What's with you not answering your phone?" he said. "I've been trying to call you for the last twenty minutes."

She groaned. "I know, I'm sorry. I thought it was my ex-boyfriend."

"Listen, Lenny is coming back to the island."

Amanda felt a shiver. "Why? When?"

"Right now. I managed to bug his phone – it was interesting, actually, because I got ahold of this hidden camera he was using, but it was a dead end. And when I was staking out the Starbucks closest to his apartment – "

"Mike, focus!" Amanda said, getting up to peek out of her window. "Do I need to hide?"

"Oh, right. No, not really. But stay home. I don't always listen to his calls right away, so I didn't realize until now. About an hour ago, he called DGG, and he was pretty angry. One of their employees was messing around on his properties. So he's going to the island to discipline him. Or kill him, I'm not sure. You need to stay away, I've been trying to get ahold of your dad but – "

"*Kill him*? Are you talking about Will?"

There was silence for a moment. "Ah. He's your boyfriend, isn't he?"

Amanda sighed. "No, he's – "

Mike cut her off. "Is he the ex-boyfriend?"

Amanda shut her eyes. "No. Neither of those things. Will is my *friend* from DGG."

"Right. Well, your relationship status is of no importance to his survival. I'm headed to the island now, but I probably won't be able to charter a flight quickly enough. I'm regretting that I sold my plane. Do you know where Will is? Can you direct him to safety?"

Panic started building in her mind, but she forced herself to quiet it. She'd be of no use if she were panicking. "I can try. Do you think he's in danger?"

"Yes."

Oh man, deep breaths. "Should I call the police? Ah, should I call my dad?"

"Yes to all of those things. And call Will. Let me know when everyone's aware."

Mike hung up and Amanda turned to Jade in terror. "Did you hear all of that?"

Jade nodded. "Mostly, though I couldn't hear everything he was saying. What's going on?"

Amanda felt dizzy. "Lenny might be trying to kill Will – I need to warn him."

Jade stared at her, eyes wide. Amanda didn't have time to waste – she called Will's phone.

No answer.

Dang it!

She tried again with the same result before sending him a text. "Please pick up, it's an emergency. You need to get to a safe place. Not your house. And not any of the properties. Maybe the police station? Lenny is coming for you. Call me."

She hit send and immediately tried calling again. Still no answer.

"Shoot!" Amanda said. "I don't know where he is."

Jade bit her lip. "Well, should we at least call the police?"

"Yeah...but what do I tell them? There's a guy in danger, and I don't know where he is, and there's another guy coming to hurt him, but we don't know where he is either?"

"Good point," Jade said, frowning. "What about your dad?"

Amanda nodded. "Right. Let me call him."

She called her dad's cell phone, also with no answer. "Ugh, nothing."

She dialed the police non-emergency line and spoke to the operator. "I'm looking for Chief Hank Kowalski. This is his daughter, Amanda."

"Oh, is everything okay? I'm afraid your dad is busy – we had a capsized passenger boat. There was a collision, and all of the deputies were called in to assist in rescue. One of the boaters fled the scene – I think your dad is tailing him."

Amanda groaned. Of course today would be the day that her dad decided to be a hero on the marine patrol.

"I can get a message to him over the radio?"

"Ah..." Amanda didn't know what to say. Lenny showing up was an emergency, but she didn't have any clue where he was, and she didn't want to leave people out in the ocean to drown. Mike would just need to call in the FBI. "Can you tell him that Lenny is coming back? Like, now. He'll know what that means."

"Sure. I'll get on the radio."

"Thank you!"

Amanda hung up, typing out a quick text to her dad with all that she knew.

Jade waited patiently. "What's going on?"

"Ugh, it's a mess. There was a boating accident. They're fishing people out of the water, and my dad is chasing someone down in a sheriff's boat."

"Let me call Matthew, he's off of work today," Jade said, stepping out of the room.

Amanda nodded, then called Mike again.

"Talk to me," he said, answering on the first ring.

"The police here are tied up with a boating accident. You're going to need to call in back up from the FBI."

"That's not an option," Mike replied. "I'm not in the FBI anymore."

"What!" She shouted into the phone. "*Now* you're telling me!? I can't find Will!"

"Well, you need to try harder."

Amanda gritted her teeth. "Thank you Captain Obvious. Which airport is Lenny flying into? Can you at least tell me that?"

"No. I would guess that he's coming by seaplane so he can't easily be spotted. San Juan hasn't been good to him. He could show up anywhere."

Amanda groaned. "We're running out of time Mike."

"Yes. Stay put, I'll figure this out."

There was one place that Will was *most* likely to be – the estate. Could she get there and warn him before it was too late?

"I'm going to look for him. I'll share my location with you."

"Amanda, no, you – "

She hung up, grabbed her car keys, and the pepper spray that Margie got her. She was already in her car when Jade called.

"Where are you going? I called Matthew – he was out for a run with Toast."

"His dog?"

"Yeah. He's going to help. What should he do, though?"

"Maybe he can go to Will's apartment to look for him? And to look for Lenny? I'm going to the estate."

"Amanda, you can't go alone! At least – "

"He's probably at his apartment. I'm just not sure, and I can't let him walk into it blind. Lenny probably doesn't know about the estate."

Jade sighed. "You don't know that."

"I have to look. Let me know what Matthew finds."

Amanda got to the estate quickly, and decided that pulling into the driveway would be foolish on the off chance that Lenny was already there.

She decided to park on the street and sneak onto the property instead. She had the advantage of knowing the layout, despite the progress that was made in the landscaping and in some of the outdoor repairs.

Amanda crept through the tall grasses as far as she could, surprised to see that there didn't appear to be anyone working on the property. Sunset was in about half an hour – perhaps they'd called it quits?

Once past the grasses, Amanda resorted to army crawling through some lower shrubs, twigs scraping her skin and crackling under her weight, until she had a clear site of the house.

She saw Will's car and felt a flutter in her chest. There didn't seem to be anyone else. She was just about to raise herself up from the ground when she heard a car cruising up the driveway.

A black SUV pulled into her view and Lenny got out of the passenger seat.

Her chest tightened. A formidable looking man got out of the driver's seat, his scowl visible even from a distance.

"Lenny, you really didn't have to come all the way out here," Will said, approaching from the house.

Lenny smiled, shaking Will's hand. "I think I did, Will. I think I did."

The second man stepped forward and threw a punch, cracking into Will from the side.

Amanda had to cover her mouth as she gasped.

Will stumbled to the ground, holding a hand up defensively. "Please – "

"What did I tell you, Will? Huh? What did I tell you?"

"I'm sorry Lenny, I'm not sure what – "

"Give me your phone. Did you do something stupid like call the police?"

Will shook his head. "No, I didn't call anyone."

Lenny grabbed the phone, smirking. "I guess you're not *that* bright."

The second man pulled Lenny aside. "Don't let him talk his way out of this. You need to show him who's in charge."

Lenny seemed to consider this for a moment. "Yeah. You're right. I'm not the kind of guy who lets people walk all over him."

In that pause, Will leapt from the ground and ran toward the house, slamming the door shut behind him.

"Great," Lenny said, turning to his companion. "Now I'm going to have to play hide and seek."

"I'll do it," the man said, taking a step toward the house.

"No." Lenny put up a hand. "I'll take care of it."

He started walking to the house, and the second guy turned around, arms crossed, facing the other direction.

Shoot. He might be able to see her if she didn't stay down. Amanda pulled out her phone – there were messages from Jade – she couldn't read those now. She sent her location and a message to Jade, Mike, and her dad. "911 – Lenny at the estate. Another guy here. Send help NOW."

Just as she hit send, a series of gunshots rang out. She looked up, terrified to see Lenny shooting at the front door of the house.

The glass shattered, and the doorknob fell to the ground with a clank. Lenny reached a hand in and pulled the door free.

"Will, I just want to talk. C'mon buddy, where'd you go?"

There was no time to waste. Amanda saw that the guard was looking away. She made a mad dash for the back of the house, diving into a muddy marsh as she rounded the corner. She crawled through the mud until she reached the back door to the kitchen.

She was going in.

Chapter 27

Will wished that he'd made it a priority to clean out the secret passageway. It was *so* dirty in there – it was making his eyes incredibly itchy.

He strained to see against the darkness. There was something on the ground. He lowered himself to examine it, then quickly shot back up.

Bones. Rat bones, maybe mice? Will wasn't sure. But he'd found where the cat liked to hang out.

Will was allergic to cats.

His eyes watered again, as if on cue. He pinched his nose. Do not sneeze. Do not sneeze. Do not sneeze.

He sneezed.

Great.

Will froze. He could hear something – it sounded like someone moving toward him. He thought that Lenny had gone upstairs, but maybe he was back? The doorway in the bookcase wasn't difficult to find, especially if Will hadn't closed it all the way...

The door on the kitchen side of the passageway quietly opened.

Game over.

Will stood there with his eyes closed, as though that would help him. If he couldn't see Lenny, then Lenny couldn't see him. Perfect logic.

He felt a tug on his arm and let out a sigh. Will opened his eyes.

It wasn't Lenny! It was Amanda, standing in the dim light. Her hair was wet and she smelled of earth, but it was definitely her. He was about to say something but she hurriedly placed her hand over his mouth.

He kept quiet. She slowly shook her head and pulled out her phone, typing a message.

"Help should be here soon. We just need to stay quiet and hide."

He smiled and reached toward her. At first, she motioned to hand over her phone, but that wasn't what he was going for. He grabbed her hand and squeezed it tightly. Amanda smiled.

Will had no idea how she'd found him, or why she'd showed up like this, but he wasn't asking questions. If Amanda said hide, he was going to hide.

They stood there in silence for what felt like hours, but was probably a matter of minutes. Lenny continued his search of the house, checking each closet and corner thoroughly. Fortunately for Will, the house was enormous.

And then, he sneezed again.

"Come on William, I'm not going to hurt you. We just need to talk. You know, man-to-man. Come on out, I know you're in here somewhere."

Will couldn't stop it. Tears pooled in his eyes as the cat dander, which he was apparently bathing in now, stung every inch of his nose.

He buried his face in his arms, but it was no use. He started to rapid fire sneeze, one after the other.

Will could hear Lenny's footsteps, running toward the library now. It would only be a matter of seconds before he saw the poorly disguised bookshelf in the library.

Will shoved Amanda, back into the safety of the darkness, just as the bookshelf flew open.

"How cute," Lenny said as he grabbed Will by his shirt and pulled him out. "You found yourself a little hiding spot."

Will tripped, falling onto the ground. He put his hands up. "Lenny, there's no need for this."

"You know what there was no need for? For you to go poking your nose where it didn't belong. You've done this to yourself."

Lenny pulled the gun from his holster and cocked it, outstretching his arm at his side. "It's too bad, Will."

"No!" Amanda screamed from behind them.

Will just barely caught the look of surprise on Lenny's face before he spun around. Amanda's arm was raised, and something shot through the air, directly into Lenny's face.

Will started coughing – what *was* that?

"Get the gun!" Amanda yelled.

Will saw that it had fallen to the ground and he rushed forward to grab it.

Lenny was on his knees, screaming. "Stop – stop! I wasn't going to do anything! I was just going to scare him!"

Amanda looked down at him and frowned. "What other weapons do you have?"

"Nothing," he said, choking. "I swear."

"Keep your voice down," Amanda said. "Or I'll spray you right in the mouth."

Lenny let out a sort of pathetic whimper, and Amanda stooped down, patting his chest, ankles, and pockets.

Will stayed on the ground, stunned and wide-eyed. How did she know how to do that? Was Amanda a...flight marshal or something? Did she know about the mob because she was involved with it, too?

No, that didn't make any sense. That couldn't possibly be it.

There was a commotion outside – yelling. Will and Amanda locked eyes for a short moment before a dog burst into the library, hackles raised. He stopped a few feet short of Lenny, barking and snarling at his face.

"Good boy, Toast," Amanda said, looking down at Lenny. "If you move, he *will* eat you."

Lenny didn't move. Neither did Will, mesmerized by the dog. For a moment he wondered if this was a bizarre nightmare.

There was more noise – it sounded like the door was kicked open.

"Police!"

"Over here Dad," Amanda called out. "I've got Lenny."

Three officers rushed into the room, guns drawn. Will put his hands up reflexively.

"That's Will," Amanda said, pointing. "He's okay. He got the gun off of Lenny."

"I don't want it," Will said, holding the gun above his head. One of the officers took it from him, then went to assist with handcuffing Lenny, who was still writhing in pain on the floor.

The third deputy hugged Amanda. He was a big guy, with a mustache and stern face. Will recognized him from a picture – Amanda's dad.

"What on *earth* were you thinking," he said to her, squeezing her tight. "You should have waited. We were on our way. Mike called me, he – "

"I couldn't wait, Dad. Lenny shot the door open, I didn't know what else he was going to do."

He pulled away, incredulous. "What was your plan? To pepper spray him to death?"

She smiled. "I didn't have a plan. I just needed to outlast him, and I did."

Will stood up, still dumbfounded, watching this exchange. It wouldn't make sense for Amanda to be in the mob – her dad was a cop. Although that would be a sort of tragic irony, like something from a movie...

"Dad, this is my friend Will. Will – this is Chief Hank Kowalski."

Will stuck out a hand and Chief Kowalski accepted it with a firm grip. Will managed to hold his own. "It's very nice to meet you, sir."

He nodded, a frown fixed on his face. "Right."

"Did you get the guy outside?" Amanda asked.

"Yep, he gave up without a fight. Matthew got him. How about we get out of here? I'm going to have to get a statement from you, again."

She smiled widely. "What do you need to know? That I'm a great shot? I heard you were stuck on a high speed boat chase. You should've brought me along – with a harpoon. I would've caught the boat for you."

"Let's go." He laughed, shaking his head. "You too, Will."

Will shook himself out of his stupor and followed behind them.

After giving an exhaustive statement to the police, Will's cell phone was returned. Along with missed calls and the strange message he got from Amanda a few minutes too late, there was an angry voicemail from Gordon telling him that he was fired.

"Everything okay?" asked Amanda, creeping toward him.

"Oh – yeah. Just had a message from my boss letting me know that he's no longer in need of my services, and that he considers my presence here to be trespassing."

Amanda's jaw dropped. "The nerve! Does he know that you were almost *killed*?"

Will shook his head. "I don't think so. He called before Lenny got here."

"Oh."

She reached toward him and he flinched.

"Sorry," she said quickly.

"No, I'm sorry. I'm still just – shaken up. You were amazing in there, though." He paused. "Are you sure you're not in the mob, too?"

She offered a weak smile and he immediately regretted verbalizing that ridiculous idea.

"Listen," she said, "I'm sorry about all of this. I should've warned you a long time ago about Lenny. I should've..." She looked down at her shoes. "I'm just really sorry about everything. I should go."

And with that, she took off, walking down the long driveway. A few moments later, Chief Kowalski followed in his patrol car.

Will was left standing there, trying to make sense of everything that had happened.

Chapter 28

Well. He wasn't dead, but he *had* lost his job. Amanda let out a sigh. How was Will's family going to get by without his income?

The manic adrenaline was clearing from her system. Now she felt low – very low. She wanted to stop driving and pull over, maybe lay out in the grass for a few hours.

She couldn't do that, though. Her dad had insisted on following her home, and if she got out and laid by the side of the road, he'd be alarmed.

No, she had to keep going. At least for a bit.

If only she'd told Will the truth about Lenny from the beginning, instead of using him like a pawn. Maybe he would've quit DGG weeks ago. He never would've ended up on Lenny's hit list. He wouldn't have wondered if she, too, was in the mob.

It was her fault. By telling him a hint of the truth, she put him in the greatest danger possible. It was her fault that he'd almost died; it would've been better if he had never met her.

When she stepped out of her car, Jade and Morgan rushed to meet her, wrapping her in a hug.

"Amanda! *What* were you thinking?"

She tried to shrug but it was hard to do in their grasp. "I don't know. I was just reacting."

"You forgot the first rule of living in this house," Morgan said, shaking a finger. "If you're going to get yourself into trouble, you *have* to bring us along with you."

Amanda laughed. "I'll remember that for next time."

"I'm pretty sure that if you attack Lenny a third time, then that's Yahtzee, right?" Jade said with a smile.

"That is *not* how that game works," Morgan responded with a snorting laugh.

"You won't have a chance to attack him again," Amanda's dad said, stepping up behind her. "The attempted murder charge is going to be much harder for him to shake."

"Well that's good," Amanda said softly.

Jade pulled back and looked at her. "Are you okay?"

Amanda nodded. "Yeah – I'm just really tired."

"And *dirty!*" Morgan said. "Did you wrestle Lenny in the mud or something?"

"Ha, no. Just pepper sprayed him," Amanda said.

"My mom would be proud," Jade added. "Okay well, do you want to get cleaned up? I'm going to throw some dinner together. My mom's on her way over – she almost had a heart attack when I told her what was going on."

Amanda smiled and agreed to the plan, though really she'd prefer to lock herself in her bedroom for the next week.

She instead made her way to the bathroom. Once the door was shut and she didn't have to pretend to be okay, Amanda looked at herself in the mirror.

She looked like a crazy person. Her clothes were caked in mud, now dried and flaking off in clumps. There was dirt all over her face and pressed into her hair.

At least she didn't have any cuts or bruises. Will would probably have a black eye after that sucker punch.

Whenever she thought about him, it made her feel dizzy. She sat down on the edge of the bathtub. She had to do something – she had to make up for some of the damage that she'd caused.

An idea hit her. Months ago, she'd worked with a financial group for an advertising campaign. Amanda became friendly with one of the women who worked there – Abby. They were about the same age and went out for drinks a handful of times while the project was ongoing. Amanda always felt too sheepish to ask her to hang out again, but she was willing to reach out for a good cause.

She pulled out her phone and wrote a long text about Will, asking if they were hiring.

Abby's answer came minutes later. "Oh my gosh, it's so nice to hear from you Amanda! Yeah actually – we are hiring. What does your friend do? We need to hang out again soon! Do you want to see the new Bond movie with me?"

Amanda smiled. They'd connected over their love of action movies – she'd love to see Abby again. Maybe they could be actual friends instead of just work friends.

She wrote back that she'd love to see the movie together, and also sent a link to Will's website. "I met him here on the island. He's been doing amazing work."

"Yeah, it looks like he could be a good fit! Tell him to apply – I'll make sure that my boss gets his resume."

Amanda smiled. She couldn't make up for what she'd done, but it was a start. She turned on the shower and stepped in, washing away the muck and the grime of the day.

Chapter 29

Rain hovered over the island like a dark omen for the rest of the week. Will felt like the continuous downpour was washing everything away – from the progress on the estate's walking paths (that he was no longer in charge of), to his hopes of a booming career in finance, and finally, to his chances with Amanda.

It had to mean something that she came back to save him, didn't it? Maybe she just felt guilty. Maybe she really *was* associated with the mob, or she was an undercover cop or something...

He didn't know. He regretted asking her if she was in the mob; that clearly made her uncomfortable. She ran off, and now he couldn't get her attention again.

He'd texted her that evening to see how she was doing. She brushed off his questions about her well-being and instead expressed how sorry she was that he'd lost his job, and that she had a lead on a new company for him.

It was exceedingly kind of her to find him a job opportunity, but also a bit confusing. Why was that her primary concern? Sure, he applied to the job – though he didn't have much hope that Gordon would provide him with a reference – but he would've preferred being able to sit down and talk to her. He wanted to acknowledge the craziness that they'd just experienced – it was crazy, wasn't it? Or was this her normal life?

He wanted to finally take her out to that dinner, but the Sunday that they'd spent sitting between the rows of lavender seemed like it was years ago.

Amanda was polite, but distant. Perhaps she and her boyfriend had gotten more serious; perhaps she just didn't like him.

Whatever the reason, it was obvious that she wanted to be left alone, and Will felt like the least that he could do was honor her wishes.

He planned to move back to his Seattle place full-time, and find someone to sublet the apartment he'd gotten on the island. He had enough savings that he could get by for at least four months without a job, but having *two* rents to pay, along with his parents' mortgage, wasn't ideal.

That week, he occupied himself with getting the apartment ready and was surprised to get a call for a phone interview from Amanda's lead.

It went well but somehow, even that couldn't cheer him up.

On Saturday evening, he decided to take his sulking to the brewery. It was packed, as usual, but he was able to get a seat at the bar.

It was there, as he stared into his beer, that he felt a tap on his shoulder.

"Will?"

He turned to see Morgan, smiling broadly. He straightened, looking around to see if Amanda was nearby. "Hey Morgan, how are you?"

"I'm good! I just did some pictures here for a surprise engagement."

"Oh, that's nice." Ah. So she probably wasn't with Amanda. He could stop looking.

"Glad to see that you're alive," she said.

"Thanks, I try. How's everything? How's...Amanda?"

Morgan let out a sigh. "Oh you know, stomping around. As she does."

"Is something wrong?"

"No, not really. She broke up with her boyfriend – well, her pseudo-boyfriend. I don't know, he was extremely annoying."

"Oh really?" Will shifted. No need to look too eager. "She...broke up with him?"

Morgan nodded, drumming her fingers on the bar. "Yeah, like *right* before she rescued you from Lenny. It seemed like she was finally going to turn her life around, but then..."

"Then what?"

"I don't know," Morgan said with a shrug. "She's been so quiet. She won't talk to me. Maybe she'd talk to you?"

He laughed. "Right. I wish."

Morgan cleared her throat, causing the man sitting next to Will to turn around. She smiled, asking, "Excuse me buddy, can you slide down?"

He shot her a puzzled look and she waved him down until he obliged.

"Just one stool, thanks so much."

Will stopped himself from laughing as he watched the man move seats.

Morgan didn't seem to notice the annoyed look she'd earned. "I'm not really one to get into other people's business," she began. "But it seemed like you and Amanda really had a great thing going. What happened?"

"Honestly, I'm not sure. She told me that she was seeing someone. And after the whole Lenny incident, it seems like she wants nothing to do with me."

Morgan narrowed her eyes. "I see."

They sat in silence for a moment until Morgan spoke again. "Because between you and me, I think she really likes you."

He turned toward her. "Really?"

She nodded. "Yeah, Amanda just isn't great with feelings. Like, honestly she's pretty bad at expressing herself."

"So how can you know?"

"I just...have a hunch."

"Ah."

She leaned in. "There's really only one way to know for sure."

He nodded. "Right. You mean we should tell her that I'm in danger and see if she comes to my rescue again?"

Morgan grabbed his arm. "I have an idea."

"Uh, I don't think we should lie to – "

"Shh! Hang on, it needs a second to come together."

Will stared at her. "Do – "

"Ssh!" After a moment she spoke again. "Okay. Yes, I definitely have an idea. The question is...how far are you willing to go?"

"I'll do anything."

Morgan smiled. "That's what I like to hear."

Chapter 30

The weekend was not off to a promising start. Amanda spent Saturday locked in her room trying to catch up on work, but ended up spending most of her time procrastinating.

Then the rain that plagued the island all week carried into Sunday morning. Amanda initially thought that she might go for a hike to clear her head, but she was not outdoorsy enough to brave the rain. That was more of a Jade move.

Amanda rolled over in bed, wondering what it would be like to spend the entire day there. She'd never done anything like that before – was now the time to start? It could be a new hobby for her – lying in bed. Maybe she'd get into reading again.

No. She could read outside of bed. Not that she *would,* but she could.

At least she had the excitement of a job interview next week. That would be something, surely. Just something to look forward to, something to keep her getting up in the morning.

With Amanda's packed schedule of nothingness, Morgan was easily able to convince her to help at the barn at Saltwater Cove. Apparently, someone had booked a last-minute engagement party and Margie needed help setting up.

Morgan had a client meeting, but sent Amanda off to get coffee for everyone that would be joining them at the barn.

When she got there, it looked deserted. She approached the barn slowly – it looked like all of the lights were off.

Amanda carefully opened a side door and slipped in, grateful to be out of the rain. It seemed that Morgan and Jade hadn't yet managed to get there. Not even Margie was there yet.

That was okay – Amanda would get started early. She liked working alone, and she enjoyed solitude.

She set the coffees down as she fumbled around, looking for the light switch, when the barn suddenly lit up. Had she bumped the switch by accident?

No, it wasn't the overhead lights that had turned on. It was the bistro lights, softly illuminating all that was beneath it.

A breath caught in her throat. The barn was decorated magnificently, with hundreds of flowers – white tulips, pink tinged lilies and rows of lavender. Music started playing over the speakers.

Amanda's pulse quickened – was this some sort of trap?

"Hello?" she called out, her voice small.

"At Last" rose from the speakers, Etta James' voice ringing out...

Her jaw dropped. In the middle of the dance floor stood Will, dressed in a tuxedo and his masquerade mask.

"Hey. I'm glad you made it."

Amanda looked around. "Will? I don't – "

"We never got to finish our dance," he said, offering his hand. "Would you mind?"

She was either completely losing her mind, or she'd been tricked. Amanda wasn't sure which was worse. Despite this internal debate, she found herself drifting toward Will, and he stepped forward to take her hand.

He pulled her in, placing his other hand on her waist. It was all too familiar, the warmth of his touch, the smell of his cologne. She was tempted to rest her head on his shoulder, but resisted.

"I like what you did with the place," she said.

"Thanks. I thought you might."

"What is this, though? Are you still stalking me?"

He smiled. "I told you – I just wanted to finish our dance. That was the night everything fell apart, wasn't it? So maybe we can start again."

"It *was* when everything started to fall apart," she said, biting her lip. "I never should've agreed to go to that ball. I'm sorry that I did."

He pulled away, cocking his head slightly. "Why?"

"Because that's when Lenny made the connection. And I told you about him, but I didn't tell you enough, and then – "

He pulled her in closer. "I don't regret any of it."

His cheek grazed hers as he pulled her closer before spinning her out.

Amanda laughed. She couldn't help it – she was dressed like she was going to dig oysters out of the mud, with holes in her jeans and an ugly sweater. Will looked like he had stepped out of a magazine.

"I wish I'd known the dress code before I came here," she said.

"You look lovely," he replied, bringing her back in. "And unlike the last ball, there's no one here to leer at you. Except me."

She rolled her eyes. "You don't really leer. That was your boss."

"Good thing I left the company, then."

"Is it?" The song ended and she stepped away from him. "If I'd never gone to the ball, maybe you wouldn't have lost your job. Or almost died. I don't know how to apologize to you, Will. It's my fault that you went to look at Lenny's properties. It's my fault that he tried to kill you. I feel awful, it's – "

"It's all about how you look at it," he said, stepping toward her. "And I don't see it that way at all."

She scoffed. "Then you're delusional."

"Maybe I am." The music picked up and he reached for her hands, playfully swinging from side to side. "The way I see it, you saved me from blindly going down a very dark career path. And I think you might've found me another job!"

She couldn't resist his dancing – he looked so goofy. "Oh, did you get an interview?"

"Yep. Already had the phone interview. Charmed the pants off of them," Will said, sticking his arm up in the air and trying to twirl himself.

She laughed as they rejoined. He was too much. "I'm glad. I'm looking for a new job, too."

"Good. Your boss doesn't deserve you. I don't think anyone does."

He attempted something too complicated – crossing their arms over their heads and spinning. Amanda released her grip. "I don't think I can do that."

He shook his head. "Of course you can. You don't have to hide that you're a trained assassin anymore."

"I'm not," she said with a laugh. "It was just that one time with the pepper spray. And the taser."

"The taser? I didn't hear about that."

She swayed with him, glad that he couldn't see the redness in her cheeks. "Lenny broke into my stepmom's house a few months ago. I happened to be there, and I happen to be really good with a taser."

He laughed. "That is wild. You have to forgive my *brief* moment where I wondered if you were in the mafia."

She sputtered out a laugh. "Really?"

"I was confused," he said, shrugging. "You're so mysterious."

"There's nothing mysterious about it. My dad – "

"I know, he's a super protective scary cop." He stopped moving and looked at her. "You're good at protecting yourself. In every way. I get it. But you should know that you've made it hard for me."

"How so?"

"Because despite all those walls of yours, I was pulled into your web from the moment I met you."

"My web!" She laughed. "That's an odd way to put it."

He paused. "The truth is, I don't care if you're in the mob. Or if you're an undercover assassin, or whatever. I just like you, Amanda. Whoever you are."

She pulled her hands away. Did Will really know what she was like? Was he making an informed decision?

"Will..."

He stared back at her. "I know that you had a thing going on, and – "

"No," she shook her head. "That's over."

"Ha, so Morgan was right. You *are* single."

She smiled. Of course Morgan was involved. "Yes, but Will – "

"I was inspired by your bravery. Not just with the pepper spray, but all the time. And I want you to know that you don't have to worry about protecting yourself from me."

She stared at him, studying the now fully outlined bruising on his face. The mask only partially hid it. "I think that you're way braver than I am."

"Oh yeah?"

"It's a lot easier for me to taser someone than to tell them how I feel."

He smiled. "I'm ready, then. Pull out your taser. If that's what you need to do to show me how you feel."

She stepped in closer. She had no desire to tase Will – nor did she want to keep running from him, or making excuses as to why he should stay away from her. "Are there any other options?"

He smiled, leaning in. "I could kiss you, if you'd prefer?"

"Yeah," she nodded, her voice almost at a whisper. "Kiss me before I find the taser."

"Gladly."

Their lips met, and though Amanda was pretty sure that they'd stopped dancing, it felt like the room was spinning. She closed her eyes, falling into his grip, a lightness overtaking her.

She snapped back to reality when Will's phone rang. Amanda pulled away. "Go ahead – answer it. It might be about your new job."

"Right." He flashed a smile. "Hello? Yeah – you're good. Well, first she threatened to taser me, but I think she's digging me now."

Amanda's mouth popped open, and almost immediately her questions were answered as Morgan, Jade, and Margie came bursting through the door, dressed up and masked. They were followed closely by her dad, Matthew – and Luke!

It took a moment before Morgan spotted Luke, standing in the back with a bouquet of flowers, but when she did, she screamed. "I thought you weren't coming for another two weeks!"

"I couldn't wait any longer," he said, wrapping her in a hug.

Amanda was too stunned to know what to say. "You were *all* in on this?"

Jade shrugged. "Well *someone* had to help you."

Amanda looked at them, astonished. "Now I really feel underdressed."

"Don't worry!" Morgan called out, stepping away from Luke. "I brought your dress. And your mask. Just, you know, in case you decided you weren't going to attack Will and we could all have a nice masquerade ball of our own."

"Ah, so that's what this is. You just wanted a chance to wear a mask."

"It does seem that way," Will said with a smirk.

Amanda didn't care. She couldn't stop smiling. Even her dad was wearing a mask; it managed to partially hide his suspicious glare at Will.

Will noticed, quickly dropping the arm that he'd had around Amanda's shoulder. "Good to see you again, Chief Kowalski."

He grunted in response, and Margie elbowed him.

"Go ahead," Margie said. "Tell them what you told me."

Amanda tilted her head. "What was it, Dad?"

He sighed. "I might've admitted that I'm a *little* impressed with what he did with the place."

Margie beamed. "See, that wasn't so hard, was it?"

Amanda laughed. Her dad relented, and shook Will's hand. "Nice to see you again too, Will."

For an absurd moment, Amanda felt like she might cry. The moment was halted, however, when Morgan screeched from across the room. "Get over here before you miss out on this '99 Red Balloons' dance-off goodness!"

Epilogue

The view from his new house was perfect; he couldn't see anyone or anything at all. It was wooded bliss, completely secluded, just the way that he liked it. No one could get within five hundred feet of the property without Mike knowing it, and considering the year he'd had, that was exactly what he needed.

Margie was convinced that he'd want his old house back, but it couldn't be further from the truth. Sure, Mike had liked that house, back in the day. But it made him too vulnerable to be on the water. His new place was much more secure, and he told her that much.

Besides, Mike wasn't going to challenge Hank and kick them out of their marital home. He was lucky that Hank didn't try to drown him after Amanda ended up in Lenny's line of fire again.

It wasn't Mike's finest moment; he could admit that now. Though he hadn't expected Amanda to go barreling into danger on her own. He also just wasn't used to working with people – non-professionals in particular. Perhaps he should've paid more attention to her romantic feelings; that would've given him a hint of what she was willing to do. It was all part of the process of getting used to living amongst regular people again.

It was odd having obligations, like Sunday dinner. He sighed as he got dressed for the event. He was never one for big gatherings – there were too many competing voices for his taste.

Yet this was life with regular people – with family. When he got to the house, he maintained his quiet for most of the dinner and watched the ones he didn't know. Tiffany had flown in from Olympia with her fiancé Sidney. He was a clean-cut sort of guy, and also a man of few words.

Mike monitored him carefully. Though he had insisted that the only people he wanted to talk to were his sister, Hank, and Amanda, Margie shot that down quickly.

"We're a *family*, Mike. You have to include everyone. Otherwise you just cause trouble and confusion, as you've seen."

"The boyfriends aren't family. I can't even do proper background checks," he complained.

Margie ignored his protests, so there he was, watching them all and scowling.

No one seemed to take much notice of him. They were focused on Tiffany and Jade announcing their plan to have a joint wedding, right at Saltwater Cove.

Margie was ecstatic. "This is the best news I've had all year!"

"Are you sure that you don't mind?" Jade asked.

"*Mind*? This is wonderful!

"And," added Tiffany, "It'll save me a lot of work in planning."

Hank nodded. "It's economical, not just with money, but with everyone's time."

Margie shot him a stern look and he retreated into his slice of apple pie. Mike caught Sidney's eyes, and they both stifled a laugh.

Maybe this guy wasn't *so* bad. Hank seemed to trust him.

"Congratulations to you all," Mike finally said, breaking his silence.

"Can we expect to see you there, then?" Amanda asked.

He smiled. It was nice that Amanda was speaking to him again. She'd given him the silent treatment, followed by an earful about his "poor communication skills" after Lenny shot up that house. "I think so, yes. I plan to stay here for a while. At least until I figure out exactly what interest a New York City mob family has on San Juan Island."

Hank laughed. "Then you're gonna be here a while."

"Wait!" Morgan held up a hand. "So you're finally admitting that Lenny *is* in the mob?"

Jade smiled. "Play it a *little* cool, Morgan."

Morgan was beside herself. "I *knew* it!"

"Don't make me regret this," Mike said as he set down his napkin. Morgan quieted and he briefly considered if he needed another piece of pie. He decided against it and kept talking. "Thanks to Will and some investigating, I know what Lenny was doing with those properties."

Now he had everyone's interest.

"Really?" Amanda leaned forward. "Because I'm dying to know."

"It appears that the Sabini family decided to get involved in real estate here to launder money."

"I knew it!" said Amanda. "I *knew* it had to be something like that."

Will sighed. "And I had no clue."

"It's a bit more complicated than that," said Mike. "What they were doing was buying cheap properties – places that were worth no more than twenty, maybe fifty thousand dollars. Condemned places. But on paper they were reporting that the properties were in top condition, pulling in millions of dollars every year."

"Right, and then they sold them to DGG for millions."

"Yes, but it was more than that. They kept the properties for so short a time, the rent couldn't be the primary source of laundering."

"But why would the investors allow it?" asked Hank.

"That's what I need to figure out. From what Will has told me, DGG is a legitimate company. So why take on these huge risks?"

There was silence. Mike frowned – he was really ruining the mood. "I don't know that yet, but I'll find out. I don't mean to kill the party here."

"You're not killing the party," said Margie, patting him on the shoulder.

Amanda sighed. "Does that mean that we're going to see Lenny here again?"

"Yeah Mike, Amanda is going to run out of weapons!" added Morgan.

Laughter rippled around the table and Mike smiled. "No, Lenny will be stuck in jail for quite some time. But whatever they're doing, I don't think they're done with it yet."

"Do me a favor, Mike," Hank said, putting up a hand. "Try not to kill any of us as you figure this out, okay?"

He laughed. "Fair deal. I'll take it."

With no immediate danger in site, Mike decided it was safe enough for him to take another slice of pie. If he was going to be on the island for a while, he might as well learn to enjoy it.

Introduction to *Saltwater Promises*

An FBI agent's work is never really done...

Mike isn't about to let a little thing like being forced into retirement stop him from investigating the mob activity on San Juan Island. Sure, it's dangerous, but he can handle it. He's about to crack the case wide open, too...then he sees *her* again and everything gets way more complicated.

Lynn Campbell loves retirement. Leaving the FBI gave her more time with her daughter and let her live out her dreams of being a full-time artist. But the mystery Mike brings into her life is irresistible, and unfortunately for her peace of mind, so is the man himself.

Soon, Mike and Lynn find themselves caught up in a case neither of them should've been working on—and in the middle of a romance they never expected. Is happily ever after possible for two retired agents in Westcott Bay? Maybe. If the bad guys don't ruin their chances...permanently...

Saltwater Promises, the final book in the Westcott Bay series, is a sweet, romantic, mature women's fiction read packed with excitement, suspense, and love. Get your copy today and get all the answers you've been waiting for!

Would you like to join my reader group?

Sign up for my reader newsletter and get a free copy of my novella Christmas at Saltwater Cove. You can sign up by visiting: https://bit.ly/XmasSWC

About the Author

Amelia Addler writes always sweet, always swoon-worthy romance stories and believes that everyone deserves their own happily ever after.

Her soulmate is a man who once spent five weeks driving her to work at 4AM after her car broke down (and he didn't complain, not even once). She is lucky enough to be married to that man and they live in Pittsburgh with their little yellow mutt. Visit her website at AmeliaAddler.com or drop her an email at amelia@AmeliaAddler.com.

Also by Amelia...

The Westcott Bay Series

Saltwater Cove

Saltwater Studios

Saltwater Secrets

Saltwater Crossing

Saltwater Falls

Saltwater Memories

Saltwater Promises

Christmas at Saltwater Cove

The Orcas Island Series

Sunset Cove

The Billionaire Date Series

Nurse's Date with a Billionaire

Doctor's Date with a Billionaire

Veterinarian's Date with a Billionaire

Made in United States
Orlando, FL
02 September 2023